The
Morning Glory
War

OTHER YEARLING BOOKS YOU WILL ENJOY:

NUMBER THE STARS, *Lois Lowry*
WHEN HITLER STOLE PINK RABBIT, *Judith Kerr*
STARRING SALLY J. FREEDMAN AS HERSELF, *Judy Blume*
AND CONDORS DANCED, *Zilpha Keatley Snyder*
LIBBY ON WEDNESDAY, *Zilpha Keatley Snyder*
THIMBLE SUMMER, *Elizabeth Enright*
ALL-OF-A-KIND FAMILY, *Sydney Taylor*
THE PUSHCART WAR, *Jean Merrill*
STRAWBERRY GIRL, *Lois Lenski*
THE SLAVE DANCER, *Paula Fox*

YEARLING BOOKS/YOUNG YEARLINGS/YEARLING CLASSICS
are designed especially to entertain and enlighten young
people. Patricia Reilly Giff, consultant to this series, received her bachelor's degree from Marymount College and
a master's degree in history from St. John's University. She
holds a Professional Diploma in Reading and a Doctorate of
Humane Letters from Hofstra University. She was a teacher
and reading consultant for many years, and is the author of
numerous books for young readers.

For a complete listing of all Yearling titles, write to
Dell Readers Service,
P.O. Box 1045,
South Holland, IL 60473.

The Morning Glory War

by Judy Glassman

A Yearling Book

Published by
Dell Publishing
a division of
Bantam Doubleday Dell Publishing Group, Inc.
666 Fifth Avenue
New York, New York 10103

If you purchased this book without a cover you should be aware that this book is stolen property. It was reported as "unsold and destroyed" to the publisher and neither the author nor the publisher has received any payment for this "stripped book."

Copyright © 1990 by the estate of Judy Glassman

All rights reserved. No part of this book may be reproduced or transmitted in any form or by any means, electronic or mechanical, including photocopying, recording, or by any information storage and retrieval system, without the written permission of the Publisher, except where permitted by law. For information address Dutton Children's Books, a division of Penguin Books USA Inc., New York, New York 10014.

The trademark Yearling® is registered in the U.S. Patent and Trademark Office.

The trademark Dell® is registered in the U.S. Patent and Trademark Office.

ISBN: 0-440-40765-6

Reprinted by arrangement with Penguin Books USA Inc., on behalf of Dutton Children's Books

Printed in the United States of America

March 1993

10   9   8   7   6   5   4   3   2   1

OPM

In memory of Judy,
who died too suddenly and too soon.

For Judy's family and friends,
who shared her joy that this book
would be published.

And for those who will meet her
for the first time through
The Morning Glory War.

World War II started for the United States on December 7, 1941, and lasted almost four years. My own personal war with Susanne Saks started on June 15, 1943, and lasted almost two weeks. Actually, it started before that, in February.

CHAPTER 1

On the first day of the new term, I woke up knowing I'd be the dumbest kid in my class and nobody would like me. I looked out the window and saw a day to match my mood. Yesterday had been one of those warm, sparkling days that sometimes come to New York in midwinter, but today it was rainy, dark and cold. I got dressed and stood in front of the mirror to do my hair. I saw a short, chubby girl with ordinary features, big brown eyes, long hair and a scared expression on her face. As I twisted my hair into two smooth braids, I practiced trying to look friendly and sure of myself. I finally had to settle for a phony smile. I kept it on my face as I walked into the kitchen, where my brother had started his breakfast.

"Why are you gritting your teeth?" Danny asked when I sat down.

"I'm not gritting my teeth," I said. "I'm smiling confidently." But I let my face relax.

"Well," he said, "I wish you luck."

"Why?" I asked, wondering why he would suddenly say something nice to me.

"I never had any trouble in school until 5B," he answered, "and that's what you're in now."

I understood. "You're just trying to make me nervous," I said. "I won't have any trouble. I'm not a nasty, mischievous boy like you."

Danny had to smile at my exact quote of his 5B teacher, Mrs. Corey. "Well, at least you won't have Gory Corey," he said.

I nodded my agreement. To everyone's relief, she had retired or something the year after Danny had her. "Even if I did have her," I said, "she'd probably think I was adorable."

I finished eating and put on my jacket and hat. I shouted, "Bye, Ma," but there was no answer. When I got to the door, I knew why. There was my mother, holding a pair of galoshes, ugly black rubber things with snaps, which she expected me to wear over my shoes.

"They'll keep your feet dry," she said.

"Nobody will be wearing galoshes," I complained.

"Somebody will. You."

"I'll be the only one."

"You and thirty-five others."

The doorbell rang. It was my best friend, Paula, calling for me. I opened the door a crack and looked at her feet. Galoshes. I slammed the door shut before my mother could see.

"See?" my mother said. "Paula is wearing galoshes."

Paula rang the bell again. "I'm coming," I shouted, struggling to pull the horrible things over my shoes. I didn't want to be late on the first day. It wouldn't be as bad as being early, but it wasn't a good idea.

"I really wish you were still in my class," Paula said as we headed down the hall. We'd been together since kindergarten. Now, in the second half of fifth grade, we were being separated. Paula got to stay in 5B-3 with all the kids we knew, and I got to be in 5B-1. "Why do you think they changed your class?" she asked.

I shrugged. "A punishment from God?"

"My brother says you're being moved into the smart class," she said, watching for my reaction. "He said there's a new rule from the Board of Education that anyone who reads above eighth-grade level has to be in the top class."

My brother had said the same thing, and all the smartest kids *were* in that class. I sighed. "I don't want to change classes. I want to be in the same class I've always been in, with you."

"The dumb class?"

"I'd rather be in the dumb class with you than the smart class with Susanne Saks and that crowd," I said.

Susanne Saks lived in my building. She was pretty, popular in school and had a brother in the service. Paula and I were regular-looking, popular only with each other and had brothers who played stickball in the street. She was the girl our mothers compared us to—unfavorably. And if that wasn't enough, Susanne was always doing the right thing. Always. It was depressing.

"It won't really be that bad for you, being in Susanne's class."

"No," I said. "She'll have perfect attendance, win all the spelling bees and star in the class play." I was still sore about last year's play, when I'd been a potato in a brown crepe-paper costume. Typecasting, my brother had said.

We'd reached the outside door when we heard Susanne calling us. "Jeannie, Paula—wait up." We exchanged looks but stopped. She looked like she was going to be in a movie, with her plaid skirt and angora sweater. She was, of course, wearing brand new white boots. And I just knew that underneath there wouldn't be one bit of white polish on the brown part of her saddle shoes. Not one bit.

"I'm so glad I found you," she said. "I hate to walk alone." She linked arms with us, and off we went into the sleety drizzle.

When we got to the gym, where classes lined up in bad weather, Paula and I smiled at each other and separated without saying a word. It felt so strange to be walking away from her with Susanne that I called out, "Paula."

She stopped and turned to face me. "What?"

But I really couldn't think of anything to say except "Wait for me at twelve o'clock."

"Sure," she answered.

"Come on," Susanne said, pulling on my arm, "you've got to meet the kids."

I still felt weird as I followed her to the place where *5B-1* was stenciled on the wooden floor of the gym. A bunch of girls ran over to say hello to Susanne. A few kids stared, but most of them ignored me. I looked around and saw some slightly familiar faces from the neighborhood and one very familiar one from my old class. Vincent DeVito, the worst boy in the fifth grade, had been moved to this class, too. It figured. Vincent was bad in school, but he was very, very smart. He was also very, very cute, and a lot of the girls in my old class had had crushes on him. We spent a few minutes kind of looking past each other, trying to figure out whether or not to say hello. Then I felt Susanne grab my hand. "Hey, everybody," she said with a Judy Garland smile, "this is my friend Jeannie Newman. She's going to be in our class this term." I couldn't believe it. Susanne had introduced me as her friend. I was immediately included in the circle of chattering girls.

"I think we're going to have Miss Handler," one of them said. I had been hoping we would. Miss Handler was young, pretty and very sweet. She was one of the few teachers in our school who seemed to like children.

"She's supposed to be nice," a girl named Helene said, "but I heard Mrs. Corey is coming back."

I almost jumped. I tried to look calm as I said, "Didn't she retire? I thought she retired."

"That's what everyone thought," Helene said, "but I heard the school secretary say she took a leave of absence because some parents complained to the principal about her."

"Oh, really?" I said calmly, hoping she didn't know she was talking about my parents.

"We're sure to get Miss Handler," Susanne said. Everyone agreed, and I sent up a silent prayer that she was right.

I was pretending to be interested in a conversation about people I didn't know when I felt someone tugging at the back of my jacket. I turned to find myself face-to-face with a fat, messy girl with long, greasy hair. Not only was she wearing galoshes, but they were at least two sizes too big. "So," she said, "you're Susanne Saks's friend." It was half a question, half a statement.

"Well," I said, "we live in the same apartment house. As a matter of fact, her apartment is directly above mine."

"Good," she said.

After a pause so long that I thought the conversation was over, she said, "I'm Maxine Gold. Susanne is the most popular girl in the class, but I'm the smartest."

"I'm Jeannie Newman," I said.

"I know. I heard."

I was finding it very hard to talk to this girl. I waited again, and when she didn't say anything, I turned away. She tugged on my jacket again. "I'm doing a study of Susanne," she said. "I mean, of her popularity. I'm trying to figure out what makes her so popular."

Now she had my interest. I'd been thinking a lot about popularity, too. "Well," I asked, "have you found out anything?"

"Plenty," she said.

"For instance?"

"For instance, have you ever noticed that she never walks alone? She'd rather walk with a jerk than be seen alone."

My cheeks burned. "What else?" I asked. But the bell rang twice—our signal to quiet down and straighten our lines.

"Meet me after school, and I'll tell you what else," Maxine said as she rushed to take her place in line behind Susanne.

"Okay," I said. "I'll see you at three."

The bell rang again, and our monitor led us upstairs to our classroom. As we walked, I was thinking about how I could become more popular. Maybe I could learn something by watching Susanne, too. Of course, I knew it helped that she was tall, slender, blonde and pretty. I remembered what I'd seen in the mirror that morning. Count me out. But some of the girls who were popular were worse-looking than I was, so what made the difference? Nice clothes seemed to help. Susanne's mother was a dressmaker, so her clothes were sensational. Maybe I could get an angora sweater for my birthday. It would be a start. But now I was beginning to understand something else. Susanne had joined Paula and me because she'd rather be seen with us than with nobody. If I couldn't be with Paula, I'd rather be alone. I was doing it all wrong. I decided to start a list as soon as I got into the classroom.

The monitor told us to take any seats; the teacher would be along in a minute. As soon as I sat down, I opened my new notebook. I wrote on the first page: *How To Be Popular.* I underlined it twice. Then I wrote: *1. Nice clothes. 2. Never be seen alone.* I stared at the page, trying to think of something else. Then, remembering how quickly I'd been accepted by Susanne's friends that morning, I wrote: *3. Have a popular friend.* I was trying to think of more when the door opened.

A tall, thin woman with silver hair and an angry face walked to the blackboard and wrote, in perfectly slanted script: *Mrs. A. Corey.* If she'd written *Mrs. A. Hitler,* I wouldn't have been more scared. I'd been worrying about being stupid and unpopular. Now I really had something to worry about. Everyone knew Mrs. Corey was the meanest, strictest and most horrible teacher in the school. She probably was also someone who held a grudge.

The teacher turned, faced the class and said, "I have, as some of you know, been on leave for the past three years. I have returned. There is so much to do. Let us start at once." She quickly arranged us in size place and assigned seats, alternating girls' rows and boys' rows. I got to sit in the first seat, third row, right in front of her desk.

I tried to look polite and attentive as Mrs. Corey outlined the term's work, but I was in a state of panic and only an occasional word came though— "nutrition . . . long division . . . South America . . . American history . . . " My attention was finally caught when I heard her mention the War Effort. By now, the war had become a familiar background to my life. I no longer had nightmares of bombs falling or enemy troops marching down our quiet Brooklyn streets. I knew the real war was being fought elsewhere. What we had was the War Effort, shortages, air-raid drills and war movies.

"In addition to continuing our collection of rubber and foil," Mrs. Corey was saying, "our school will be sponsoring a newspaper-collection drive." She walked over to an oaktag chart hanging on the bulletin board next to her coat closet. "We will record each student's contribution with a bar on this graph, and at the end of the term, a real medal will be awarded to the person who has collected the most newspapers."

Everyone started talking at once, but Mrs. Corey silenced us with a look. "I have even more wonderful news," she said when we were quiet. "All the fifth- and sixth-graders in our school will be taking part in a nationwide project to raise the morale of our boys in the service. A pen-pal program is being set up between schoolchildren and servicemen overseas, so that they will get plenty of mail to keep their spirits up. How many of you would like to do that?" Every hand went up. "In a few weeks you will be given the name and address of your pen pal. We will discuss it further then."

The morning passed without any trouble between Mrs. Corey and me. Even when she called the roll, she didn't seem to notice my name. I started to relax a little. Mrs. Corey taught us the words to some songs we'd have to sing in the fifth-grade assembly; she passed out crayons and drawing paper; she gave us a list of school supplies we'd need; but it all passed over me like background music because in my head I was writing a letter to a serviceman, something that would keep him cheerful and wanting to go on.

When the bell rang for lunch, I couldn't wait to find Paula. She'd heard about the pen-pal program, too.

"I hope I get a sailor," she said. "Do you think they really want to get letters from kids?"

"Sure," I said, "the idea is for them to get tons of mail."

"What'll I write about?" Paula moaned. "Nothing ever happens to me."

"I'm going to start keeping a notebook," I said, "and write down ideas, maybe jokes."

We walked a few steps without talking. "I almost forgot," Paula said. "I got Handler. She's great. Who did you get?"

"Corey," I said, watching her face.

"You're lying," she said. "Corey retired."

"It was just a leave of absence."

"Oh, no. Is she as bad as they say?"

"Well, she's pretty strict, and she never uses contractions," I said, "but she doesn't seem that terrible. It might not be so bad. In fact, I think it's going to be all right."

I was wrong.

That afternoon, after we'd filled out book labels, filled inkwells and heard instructions on the use and care of textbooks, Mrs. Corey said, "Take out your notebook and a pen and place them on your desk." We did. "This notebook is for classwork only," she continued. "There will be another one for homework. Do not ever, I repeat, ever, write anything in your classwork notebook except what I tell you to. Is that understood?"

"Yes, Mrs. Corey," the class chorused.

"Now, open to the first page."

I did, and saw written there *How To Be Popular.* I started to tear the page out as quietly as I could, but the sound of it in that silent room was like a crack of thunder on a summer night.

"You are never to remove pages from your notebook," Mrs. Corey said, glaring right at me. "Never." She paused for a moment. "I will now show you what I want written on that first page. You," she said, pointing at me, "bring your notebook here so I can demonstrate."

I couldn't let her see that page. If she read it to the class, I'd be finished. I ripped, and the page came out. I could hear some kids gasp. Mrs. Corey held out her hand, and I gave her the notebook.

"I will have the page, too," she said.

Imagination failed me. I couldn't think of anything else to do. I just didn't have the nerve to rip up the page in front of her. I folded it and handed it to her. She placed it in her desk drawer without opening it. "And who might you be?" she asked.

I stared at her blankly. I didn't know how to answer the question.

"Your name?" she shouted.

"Jean Newman."

"Daniel Newman's sister?"

"Yes."

"Of course," she said. "I might have known. Well," she said softly, pausing between each word, and almost hissing, "we shall see."

Later, when I told Paula about it on our way home from school, she said it didn't sound that bad, but anyone who was in that room and heard her say "Well, we shall see" in that voice would know why I felt a shiver go down my back.

"Maybe you should try to get moved out of her class," Paula suggested.

"My parents would have to go in and see her," I said, "and I'm sure she has it in for them already. Then what if after that, the principal said no? I'd be in worse trouble than I am now."

"Well, you're not exactly teacher's pet now, are you?"

"No. Susanne is, of course, and this kid, Maxine Gold, who's supposed to be the smartest—oh, no."

"What?"

"I was supposed to meet Maxine after school, and I forgot." I looked back up the street to see if Maxine was still there. She was, and she was looking right at me. I started to walk toward her, but she turned and walked away.

CHAPTER 2

At the beginning of the second week of school, I discovered another way to be popular. I became a celebrity.

My mother sent me across the street to Mrs. Gruber's grocery to get some sour pickles and sauerkraut, so I was carrying two clean jars in a paper bag when I walked into the store. It was a small, narrow store, with cans and boxes lining three walls. Mrs. Gruber was standing behind the counter, which ran across the back, waiting on a woman I'd never seen before. The customer was wearing a purple coat and red shoes with very high heels. There was a pile of groceries on the counter between them.

"You can't slice the cheese any thinner?" the woman was asking in a whiny voice. "No, not *that* box of cornflakes," she said. "I want the one behind it." When Mrs. Gruber cut a chunk of sweet yellow butter for her, she said, "It's sour. Keep it."

Mrs. Gruber noticed me waiting with my jars. "Jeannie," she said, "help yourself. This may take a while. Give me your jars, and I'll weigh them."

"You're waiting on her before me?" the woman said. "I can go to the A&P, you know."

"This will only take a second," Mrs. Gruber said. Turning so only I could see her, she raised her eyebrows and made a little face. She placed my jars on the scale and wrote something on a piece of paper. Later, when the jars were full, she'd subtract their weight.

"Anything else?" she asked the woman.

I took my jars, walked to the pickle barrel and raised the lid. The tangy smell made my mouth water. The pickles were just the way I liked them, grayish and very sour. I filled the jar with as many pickles as I could squeeze in. Then I opened the sauerkraut barrel. Perfect again, not too white; this sauerkraut had been around for a while. I packed the second jar. After the jars were weighed, I'd use the cups hanging from the barrels to fill in the remaining spaces with pickle and sauerkraut juice. I walked to the counter to pay.

Mrs. Gruber was using a stubby pencil to write the prices of the woman's order on a brown paper bag. She added up the columns, her lips moving silently. "Four seventy-nine," she said, as she loaded the groceries into the bag.

The woman took out her change purse. "I forgot coffee," she said. "A pound of Maxwell House, percolator grind."

Mrs. Gruber used her long reaching stick with the two prongs to get the coffee down from a high shelf. She poured it into the grinder at the end of the counter and switched the noisy machine on. Just then, the woman grabbed her package and ran. I'd never seen a grown-up run so fast.

"Mrs. Gruber," I shouted.

She turned and understood in a second. She ran out from behind the counter, pulling her apron off as she went. She threw the apron at me, shouted, "Watch the store" and flew into the street after the woman.

I ran to the door and looked out. Mrs. Gruber, in her old-lady black oxfords, with a hole cut out for her bunion, was half a block behind the woman, but as they got near the corner, I could see that she was catching up. Then they turned the corner, and I couldn't see them anymore.

I went back inside. A few minutes must have passed before I looked at the apron in my hand and realized that I was in charge of the grocery store. I could wait on customers. I could slice cheese. I could look inside the cash register. I put the apron on and walked behind the counter.

I prayed that someone I knew would come in and see me. I sliced a piece of American cheese. I ate it. I adjusted the machine to a wider setting and sliced a thicker piece of cheese. I weighed my pickles and sauerkraut, wrote down the weight, then filled the jars with juice, inhaling deeply. I opened the door and looked out. The street was almost deserted. I walked back and pressed the No Sale button on the cash register and admired the neat arrangement of bills and coins in the drawer. I walked to the door again and saw Fat Sophie lumbering around the corner. I knew she was heading for the grocery store because that was the only place she ever went. I ran behind the counter and waited.

Fat Sophie walked in, slammed the door and stared at me.

"What are you doing here?" she said angrily. "Where's Gruber?"

Sophie was excitable, so I just said, "Mrs. Gruber had to go out for a few minutes. She left me in charge."

"You?" Sophie asked, wrinkling her brow.

"Me," I answered. I didn't want to lose my first customer, so I smiled and said, "Can I help you with anything?"

There was a long pause. Sophie looked around. She scratched herself. "Give me a small cream cheese," she said finally. I opened the dairy case and took a cream cheese out of the wooden cheese box. "A quart milk," Sophie said. I stood the cold bottle on the counter and waited. I knew she hadn't come in for cream cheese and milk. She looked around again. "Oh," she said, as if she'd just remembered, "I'll have five boxes Mallomars." I got them. That was it. Sophie ate five boxes of Mallomars every day. It was common knowledge.

I got a paper bag and a pencil and added. "One forty-five," I said.

"Put it on the book," Sophie said as I packed up her order. It was where Mrs. Gruber wrote what people owed her when they were short of money. I took out the tattered notebook and looked up Berger, Sophie's last name. There was only an Anna Berger listed. Sometimes first names were used, so I checked the *S* page. Nothing.

"You're not in the book," I told Sophie.

"I am," she said. "Ask Gruber." She picked up her groceries, turned and walked out. I found a slip of paper and wrote *Sophie—$1.45.*

Then two women I didn't know came in, and I filled their orders easily. It was like playing store, only better.

Mrs. Saks, Susanne's mother, came in. She asked me why I was there, and I explained what had happened.

"I wonder what happened to Mrs. Gruber," she said.

I filled two bags of groceries for Mrs. Saks, even remembering to collect ration stamps for sugar and butter. When she left, the store was empty again, and I started to worry about Mrs. Gruber. She was pretty old. She could have fallen or had a heart attack.

The door to the store opened again. It was Susanne. "My mother told me you were here," she said. "Do you need any help?"

"Not in the store," I said, "but maybe you could find out what happened to Mrs. Gruber."

"Okay," she said. As soon as I'd told her what

the woman looked like and which way they'd run, she left, and I was alone again.

The next customer turned out to be my mother. "How do you do?" she said. "You look a lot like my daughter, who is missing." I told her what had happened. "So," she said when I'd finished, "Mrs. Gruber trusted you with her store. I'm impressed."

"She didn't have a lot of choices," I reminded her.

"Still," my mother said.

"I'm worried about Mrs. Gruber," I said.

She walked to the door and looked out. "You can stop worrying," she called back to me. "Here she comes."

I joined my mother at the door in time to see a raggle-taggle parade coming down the dark street. In the lead was Mrs. Gruber, clutching a torn bag of groceries. She was followed by Susanne, some kids and a few grown-ups.

As she got closer, I could see that Mrs. Gruber's hair was wild, her cheeks were bright pink and she was out of breath. But she was grinning when she walked in, followed by the crowd. "I knew about this woman," she said when she finally caught her breath. "At least I knew there was a woman doing this in other stores, so I was keeping an eye on her. I should never have turned around to use the coffee grinder. If not for Jeannie, I would never have been able to catch her."

"But who was this woman?" my mother asked Mrs. Gruber.

"I don't know," Mrs. Gruber answered. "She's married to a rich dentist. It's not for the money. She told the cops she doesn't know why she does it."

"The cops?" I said.

"Sure. Someone called them when we were fighting for the groceries on Ocean Parkway."

"You ran all the way to Ocean Parkway?"

"I had to," Mrs. Gruber said. "She had my groceries."

"So what happened with the cops?"

"They brought us to the police station. That's what took so long. The cops had to call her husband."

The crowd started to break up. "You can go home now," Mrs. Gruber told the stragglers. "The show's over."

The kids I knew all came over to say, "So long, Jeannie" or "See you in school tomorrow."

When the last one was gone, Mrs. Gruber turned to me and said, "So, how's business?"

"Not too bad."

"You had customers?"

"Yes."

"You knew what to do?"

"I figured it out."

"You took cash?"

"Yes."

"You made change?"

"Yes."

"Did you remember to get ration stamps?"

"Yes."

She held out her hand. "The apron, please."

I took the apron off and handed it to her. "One thing," I said, "Fat Sophie charged a dollar forty-five, but I couldn't find her name in the book."

"What do you mean you couldn't find her name? You're a smart girl."

I shrugged.

She took out the book and leafed through it. "Here," she said, pointing.

I went behind the counter to look. There it was, under *F* for *Fat Sophie.*

"Go ahead," Mrs. Gruber said. "Finish your job. Write it in."

I wrote *$1.45* in the book.

"You're a good girl, Jeannie," Mrs. Gruber said. "Thank you, and you're fired. Go home. It's time for supper." I squeezed her hand and walked to the door.

"Wait," she shouted. I turned. "You forgot your pickles and sauerkraut. No charge."

I picked up the package and walked out. As I walked down the block to my house, the streetlights came on.

I always thought it was a good sign—good luck or something—to see the streetlights come on. I was thinking about how the kids in the store had gone out of their way to say good-bye to me, as if they wanted everyone to know that they knew me. They'd be sure to talk about it in school. I wondered what the other kids would say when they found out I was the girl who got to mind the store. I promised myself not to act like a big shot. For the first time that term, I couldn't wait for school to start the next day.

CHAPTER 3

The next morning, on our way to school, I told Paula The Amazing Story of Gruber the Grocer and the Stolen Packages. She couldn't believe she'd missed the whole thing and asked a million questions. Paula was a very satisfying best friend.

The minute I got to my line in the schoolyard, kids started coming over to talk to me. Susanne had gotten there early and told the story to everyone she met. Of course, she made it sound as though the important part had been finding Mrs. Gruber, but I was still getting more attention than she was. Kids I didn't even know came over to ask me questions; kids I hardly knew acted as if they were my friends. I felt flushed and puffed up with the attention, but I tried not to act stuck-up. Now I knew for sure why I'd wanted to become popular. It was a lot of fun.

My excitement about being famous lasted until we got upstairs. Then it was replaced by something even more exciting. "Boys and girls," Mrs. Corey said, "I have good news. I have just been given the list of servicemen who wish to receive mail from home. I will be giving out the names and addresses today. . . ." Her voice droned on, but I was so impatient that I was ready to jump out of my seat. I wondered whether I'd get a soldier, sailor or marine. Would he be serving in the Pacific or Europe? I was kind of hoping for a sailor serving in the Pacific because I'd just seen a movie about a real cute one named Joey. But really, that wouldn't matter . . .

Then I heard Mrs. Corey announce, "Health inspection," and I was immediately back in the classroom. Mrs. Corey had a monitor for everything: a blackboard-erasing monitor, a blackboard eraser-cleaning monitor, a wardrobe monitor, a window monitor, an inkwell monitor. She had a health-inspection monitor for each row. Maxine was the monitor for my row, even though she was pretty messy herself. I don't know how she got the job because her hair always looked as if it needed to be washed, and her fingernails were probably grimy, too. Her job was to check that we had a handkerchief, clean nails and polished shoes. She was supposed to ask us if we'd had a good breakfast and brushed our teeth. Only a moron would have said no, but she asked every single day.

She was also supposed to check that our ears were clean, but that was too disgusting even for Maxine. The other health-inspection monitors just went through the motions, more or less checking off everything on their charts. Maxine inspected. It was a nasty job, but she brought a lot of spirit to it.

That morning, when Mrs. Corey called for health inspection, I realized I'd forgotten my hanky and was trying to borrow one from a girl in the next row before Miss Health Inspection reached me. I was saved by the air-raid drill alarm. *Bong,* pause, *bong, bong, bong.* We lined up quickly and marched out into the hall, where we sat with our backs against the wall, away from windows and glass doors. Miss Hoffman, the music teacher, stood up in the middle of the corridor and said, "Let us do what the brave people of England do when they are in real air raids. Let us sing. We will start with 'Anchors Aweigh.' "

I was glad to be singing because it was hard to worry while you were singing. These drills were a nice break from schoolwork, but they always made me a little nervous. Everyone said Brooklyn would never be bombed, but, like all schoolchildren, I wore an ivory-colored disc on a string around my neck. It was for identification, in case we were found wandering the streets after an air raid. Mine said, in blue script:

Jean Newman

2-8-32

35-10398 N.Y.C.

I kept playing with the disc as I sang, but this time I couldn't concentrate on the bombing of Brooklyn or the song. I was thinking of my serviceman, my pen pal, when I heard Miss Hoffman shouting. "That boy," she was saying, pointing at someone I couldn't see, "stand up."

The song fizzled out, and I saw Vincent DeVito slowly getting to his feet. "And you are?" Miss Hoffman asked him.

"I am?" Vincent asked. Then he smiled his famous crooked smile. "I am wondering why you told me to stand up."

I knew Vincent well enough to realize that he was teasing her, but you could see that Miss Hoffman wasn't sure whether he was fresh or dumb.

"What is your name?" Miss Hoffman said very slowly.

"Vin-cent De-Vi-to," he answered even more slowly, looking her right in the eye.

There were some giggles, but Miss Hoffman still didn't seem sure. "Were you throwing spitballs?" she asked.

"No, ma'am," Vincent said. "It would be unpatriotic to throw spitballs during an air-raid drill."

"Well, sit down and don't do it again," Miss Hoffman said.

"I can't not do it again because I didn't do it in the first place," Vincent was saying when the all-clear sounded.

When we returned to our classroom, Mrs. Corey told Vincent that if he got in trouble one more time, she'd write something on his permanent record card. Then she went right into a lesson on the difference between a business letter and a friendly letter, with a lot of boring stuff about salutations and headings. She forgot all about health inspection and told Maxine to sit down when she got up to finish her job.

It wasn't until after lunch that she got around to talking about our pen pals again. "Some of you," she said, "will be addressing your letters to APO New York and some of you to APO San Francisco. Does anyone know what that means?" Every hand went up. "Susanne?" Mrs. Corey said.

"APO New York is the post office for servicemen in Europe, and APO San Francisco is for men serving in the Pacific," Susanne said.

"Correct," Mrs. Corey said.

Susanne's brother, Buddy, was serving in Europe, and it worried her a lot. I had seen Mrs. Saks with the women who waited downstairs for the mailman. He would open the shiny brass panel of mailboxes with his key and quickly sort the mail into the slots, sometimes handing one of the thin V-mail envelopes to the mother or wife of a serviceman. When he was finished, the women moved toward each other. Those who had mail told those who didn't that surely they would hear soon; the mails were so slow.

"Before I distribute the names," Mrs. Corey went on, "we should discuss the kinds of letters we will be writing." The discussion seemed to take hours. I was so impatient I kept squirming in my seat. I heard ". . . spelling . . . grammar . . . sports . . . hobbies . . . tell about your school . . . penmanship . . . legible . . ."

Finally, I heard Mrs. Corey say, "Please do not take a name if you are not going to write." The names were passed out on little slips of paper. Mine was Pvt. Timothy Haywood. His address was a series of numbers and letters ending with APO San Francisco. So I had half my wish. He was a soldier, not a sailor, but he was serving in the Pacific. What a great name, Timothy Haywood. It sounded like a movie star. I wondered if he was called Tim or Timmy, or maybe Woody, short for Haywood. No matter how I tried, I could only picture him looking like Joey in the movie. I spent the rest of the afternoon thinking about what to write.

At three o'clock I ran to meet Paula. "Did you get your pen pal?" I asked.

She showed me her slip of paper. Hers was Pvt. Horace Klitzer, and his APO was New York. I could tell she was a little disappointed.

"Names don't mean anything," I said. "He's probably very cute."

"I know," she said. "What are you going to write?"

"I'm still thinking about it," I answered. "I know it should be something cheerful, though."

We went together to buy V-mail stationery, tissue-thin paper in a red-white-and-blue-bordered envelope. As soon as I got home, I went into my room and wrote:

Dear Timothy,

My name is Jeannie Newman. I go to school
in Brooklyn, New York. Some people say that
servicemen like to get mail, even if it's from
people they don't know. I hope that's true. If it's
not, well, I'm sorry for the trouble, and just don't
answer.

I guess from the address that you're probably
somewhere in the Pacific. That makes me think of
Dorothy Lamour in a sarong, but it must be very
scary to be there in a war. I know that you can't tell
me anything about it because the censor will take it
right out. They're always telling us here that loose
lips sink ships. Topps Gum has posters up everywhere
that say: *Don't talk, chum—Chew Topps Gum.* That's
not my favorite sign, though. Once, when my Uncle
Benny—he's my father's favorite brother—took us out
to the country in his laundry truck, I saw this one on
the road: *Don't stick your elbow out so far. It might go
home in another car. Burma Shave.*

A lot of people at home forget that there's a war
on and grumble about the shortages. Now we have
Meatless Tuesdays. Butcher shops are going to be
closed on Tuesdays for the duration. My father says
the duration will probably last longer than the war.
Ha-ha.

Well, I see I'm running out of space. I'll just tell
you a little bit about myself and then sign off.

My favorite day is Saturday. That's the day my
best friend, Paula, and I go to the movies. When
my mother says, "You're not going to sit in a dark
movie on a beautiful day," I remind her we always
go to the movies on Saturday. I can't control the
weather—ha-ha. My mother says the movies are
ruining me, making me more dreamy and forgetful

than I already am. She says I never listen when the movie madness is upon me.

My favorite actor is John Garfield. My favorite actress is Vivíen Leigh. My favorite movie is *Gone with the Wind*. My favorite book is *Under the Lilacs* by Louisa May Alcott. My favorite radio program is "The Jack Benny Show," although I like "Fibber McGee and Molly" a lot, too, especially when Fibber opens his closet and all that junk falls out. That gets me every week.

I hope you'll write back, and I hope the war isn't too hard on you.

                              Yours truly,
                              Jeannie

I ran out and mailed the letter as soon as I finished writing it.

CHAPTER 4

Right then, I started to wait for an answer. I checked the mail when I came home from school every day and stood with the women at the mailboxes on Saturdays. I questioned the kids in my class every couple of days to make sure no one else had received a letter. No one had. For some reason, I hadn't told my mother about my pen pal. I wondered what she would think if the letter from Timothy came while I was in school. I smiled to myself when I pictured her looking at the envelope from overseas and trying to figure it out.

Things were going from bad to worse at school. Mrs. Corey picked on me. Everyone said so. She never called on me when my hand was raised, but if she saw me looking out the window or daydreaming, she'd ask me to answer a hard question. It became a game for me to pretend not to be paying attention when I was sure of an answer. It really got on her nerves when I answered it right.

The only thing that saved me from her a little was Vincent DeVito. She didn't like me at all, but she hated him. Vincent didn't follow any rule he didn't feel like following. He had a swagger and a crooked little smile, and he really didn't seem to care at all what happened to him.

Even though he had a strange way of pronouncing some words, he was still the smartest boy in the class. Vincent had always been nice enough to me, but he hung around with a crowd that was kind of tough. Not everyone liked him the way I did. I think some of the kids were a little in awe of someone who could be so smart and act so bad.

He wasn't afraid of anything, not even Mr. Fieldstone, the principal. I couldn't imagine anyone not being afraid of Mr. Fieldstone; even the teachers were. He was a strict-looking old man with perfect posture, a long, narrow nose and no lips. His eyes, hair and suit were dark gray. His voice was so loud and deep, it reminded me of thunder. My picture of God was Mr. Fieldstone in a long white robe, carrying lightning bolts. Most of the kids I knew would cheerfully accept any punishment rather than be sent to his office.

Mrs. Corey had pets, too. They were, of course, Susanne Saks and Maxine Gold. Maxine, aside from being the smartest girl in the class—Vincent was the smartest boy—was the kind of kid who reminded the teacher when she forgot to give homework. She didn't really have any friends. I mean, who could like a drip like her? Even Susanne didn't care for her. But she'd link up with Maxine if she needed somebody to do something mean. Susanne had almost everyone fooled; she was their darling.

So that was the way it was, and we all accepted it. In fact, things stayed pretty calm until the day of the spelling bee. Maxine was the best speller in the class, and Susanne, who wasn't a natural speller, studied so hard that she wasn't far behind. Between them, they'd won every spelling bee since the beginning of the term. Vincent couldn't spell, smart as he was. Forget "*i* before *e* except after *c*." He spelled *wouldn't* W-O-O-D-E-N-T. I thought it was cute. In fact, I was starting to think a lot of things about Vincent DeVito were cute.

This particular spelling bee had gone into the final rounds with me still in it, which was unusual. At the end, Maxine, Susanne and I were the only ones left. Maxine got an easy word and spelled it easily. "*Command,* C-O-M-M-A-N-D, *command.*" She was the type of girl who would never forget to say the word before and after spelling it.

Susanne's next word was *luxury*. Not simple, but no big surprise either.

My word was *conscientious*. I stood on tiptoe to see if it was really on the list, but Mrs. Corey raised the paper and held it close to her chest, probably thinking I was trying to cheat. I had been reading about conscientious objectors in the newspapers, so I knew the word and spelled it correctly.

Mrs. Corey sniffed and gave Maxine her next word, *academy*. Maxine spelled it A-C-A-D-A-M-Y

33

and was out. Mrs. Corey patted Maxine's shoulder as she returned to her seat. "Good try," she said.

Only Susanne and I were left. I suddenly wanted to win very badly.

"Susanne," Mrs. Corey said, "your next word is *laboratory*. The scientist worked in his laboratory." She pronounced the word very clearly, but Susanne just stared at her. The room was silent. "It may help you to know, dear," Mrs. Corey said, "that the English pronounce it 'la-BOR-a-tory.' "

"Oh," Susanne said. "*Laboratory*, L-A-B-O-R-A-T-O-R-Y, *laboratory*."

"Correct," Mrs. Corey said, beaming at her. "Good work." Her expression changed as she turned to me. "Your word," she said, "is *rhododendron*. In the spring, the rhododendron come into flower."

I knew *rhododendron* wasn't on the fifth-grade spelling list. I had never even heard the word before. I was furious. Mrs. Corey was cheating on a spelling bee to make Susanne win and me lose. I smiled at her, a big, fake smile. "Mrs. Corey," I said, "would you happen to know how the English pronounce that?"

I heard a gasp from somewhere in the room. Nothing at all seemed to happen for several seconds. Then I heard the nervous laughter start, stifled but loud enough. Mrs. Corey turned red, almost purple. "Maxine," she said, in a small, tight voice, "take this person to Mr. Fieldstone's office. He will know how to deal with her."

I followed Maxine into the hall and down two

flights of stairs like a zombie. My heart started to pound as we came to the double glass doors of the main office. Miss Grant, Mr. Fieldstone's secretary, was typing at her desk. Maxine spoke to her and left. Miss Grant told me to take a seat and went on typing. By now, my knees were so weak I almost collapsed into the chair.

A parent came out of Mr. Fieldstone's office, and I was sent in. I stood there, not sure if I should sit down. Mr. Fieldstone acted as if he didn't know I was there. He read a mimeographed paper, straightened some books on his desk, looked for something in a neat stack of papers, found it, read that. Finally, he looked straight at me. "Well?" he asked in that booming voice.

I jumped. "Mrs. Corey sent me here," I said. My own voice sounded strange to me, weak and thin.

"Yes," he said impatiently. "*Why* did she send you here?"

I told him. I was determined not to cry, but my voice kept cracking, and I had to keep swallowing hard. When I'd finished, Mr. Fieldstone seemed to have some kind of coughing spell. He turned away from me and looked at something in the bookcase behind him while he was making these strange choking noises. When he turned back to me, he said, "You asked her how the English pronounce *rhododendron*?"

"Yes." I knew it was crazy, but it almost seemed to me that he was struggling not to smile.

"And what did she say?"

"She sent me here."

"And do you know why she sent you here?" he asked loudly. The little sparkle I thought I'd seen in his eyes was gone.

"It was the worst punishment she could think of," I said. This time I could see the laugh start before he had a chance to turn around and pretend to choke.

When he finally turned back to me, he said, "Mrs. Corey is a three-star mother. Do you know what that means?"

It took me a moment to understand what he was saying. I'd never thought of Mrs. Corey having any life outside of the classroom, much less being a mother. Then I pictured the little satin banners that mothers of servicemen hung in their windows, with one blue star for each son in the armed forces; sometimes there was a gold star for a son killed in the war. "Yes," I said slowly. "It means she has three sons in the service."

"That makes her a little nervous at times," Mr. Fieldstone continued. "We must all show her respect and consideration." He started to look for something in the pile of papers on his desk, so I stood there, waiting for my punishment. "You may go," he said.

"What should I tell Mrs. Corey?"

"Just tell her that I talked to you. And if you could look as terrified as you did when you came in here, that would be nice." I smiled, and he smiled back at me. "Better yet," he said, "I'll walk back with you and tell Mrs. Corey myself."

When we got back to the classroom, Mr. Fieldstone opened the door and just stood there until the class jumped up and singsonged, "Good morning, Mr. Fieldstone."

"Good morning, class," he said, in his harshest voice. There wasn't a trace of a smile anywhere about him. I was having no trouble looking scared again. I began to wonder if the last ten minutes had really happened. "Mrs. Corey," Mr. Fieldstone said, "I have had a talk with this young lady which I do not think she will soon forget."

Mrs. Corey nodded triumphantly. "Thank you, Mr. Fieldstone," she said, and he turned and left.

As I walked back to my seat, I tried for an expression on my face that I'd seen in the movies on American prisoners of war returning to their cells after being tortured by the enemy. It said: Don't worry about me. I can take it. I must have gotten it right because Vincent DeVito made the thumbs-up sign and winked at me as I sat down.

On my way home from school, I was telling Paula what had happened when I heard my name being called. I turned to see Maxine and Susanne walking a little behind us. I expected them to ask about my visit to the principal, but instead Maxine shouted, "Sore loser." Susanne didn't say anything, but it wasn't hard to guess that she'd put Maxine up to it.

I couldn't believe it. "Teacher's pets," I shouted back. I made a snowball out of some hard, dirty snow left from the last storm and threw it as hard as I could in their direction. There was some squealing, but not the crying I'd been hoping for.

When I got home, my mother was out. She'd left the door unlocked and milk and cookies on the kitchen table. I was glad to be alone in the house. I needed time to decide whether or not to tell my parents about being sent to the principal's office.

I took the mailbox key off the hook in the kitchen and walked to the mailboxes. There was something in our box. I pulled out a creased and rumpled V-mail envelope and stood there for a while, turning it over and over in my hands, hardly able to believe it was real. I studied the neat hand-writing in blue ink on the thin paper, the huge army postmark on the front. I heard someone coming into the building and stuffed the letter in my pocket. I walked slowly back to the apartment, through the living room and into my room. I closed the door and took the letter out and looked at it again. It seemed so strange to see my name written in his handwriting. I stared at it for a long time before I opened it.

CHAPTER 5

I sat on the bed and read the letter for the third time. I felt as if I had a fever. It said:

Dear Jeannie,

The people who told you servicemen like to get mail, even from someone they don't know, were right. At least, I do. But the thing is, I feel like I know you. I picture you about fifteen or sixteen, small, blonde and cute. Are you a cheerleader at your school? You sound like you are.

I'm eighteen. I come from a small town in Kansas called Dayton. My father died when I was a baby, and I don't have any brothers or sisters. My mom writes to me a lot, but it's mostly about how she's praying for me and Jesus loves me and all of that. I don't know why, but her letters kind of get me down.

Boy, was it good to hear about how things are at home, about "Fibber McGee and Molly" and road signs and shortages and movies. That's what we miss here. I read your letter to some of the guys, and they all think you must be a doll. They want to know how I got so lucky.

I'm not allowed to tell you where I am or what we're doing here, but I'll tell you a little bit about what this place is like. I'm sure the censors will let this pass. XXXXXXXXXXXXXXXXXXXXXXXXXXX
CENSORED
XXXXXXXXXXXXXXXXXXXXXXXXXXXXXXXXXX
CENSORED
XXXXXXXXXXXXXXXXXXXXXXXXXXXXXXXX

Morale is really good in my unit. We kid around and do a lot of practical jokes and stuff. Yesterday we nailed this guy's footlocker closed. He almost went crazy when he tried to open it for inspection. I guess it sounds dumb to you, but making time pass is the biggest problem here.

Please write again and tell me about things at home. Nothing would be boring to me, no matter how ordinary it might seem to you. Now I'll tell you my favorites.

Actress:	Rita Hayworth
Actor:	Clark Gable
Movie:	*Angels Over Broadway*
Book:	I don't read books that much.
Radio Program:	"Inner Sanctum" and "Fibber McGee and Molly"

WRITE SOON!

Love,
Tim

My mind was going in two directions at once. I was thrilled that my letter had been such a hit and made him think I was an adorable teenager, but I felt nervous, too. I hadn't meant to make him think I was someone else. I couldn't imagine how to answer this letter, whether to just go along with it and see what happened or to tell the truth. Neither idea seemed that great. I didn't want to pretend to be someone I wasn't; I wasn't even sure I could get away with it if I wanted to. What did I know about small, blonde, cute teenage cheerleaders? And if I told the truth, that would probably be the end of my pen pal.

After thinking about it for half an hour and getting nowhere, I decided I needed advice. I certainly couldn't talk to my mother. She'd wonder why I hadn't mentioned it before. She might even think that I'd purposely tried to make him believe that I was older. There was no doubt what her advice would be, anyway. I would have to humiliate myself and tell him I was a baby fifth-grader.

The only one I could turn to was Paula. She could be trusted not to blab, and even my mother said she had common sense. I folded the letter and put it back in my pocket, grabbed my coat and ran out. I passed my mother and brother as they were coming in. "Going to Paula's," I said as I raced past them.

I must have pounded on Paula's door because she asked, "What's the matter?" as she opened it.

"Paula," I asked as soon as I got inside, "have you heard from Horace?"

"Horace who?"

"Horace, your pen pal."

"No. Why? Have you heard from yours?"

I handed her the letter and said, "Read this."

She did. "Wow," she said.

"I know," I answered.

"He signed it *Love,*" she said with a sigh.

"Paula, don't get moony on me. I came to you for advice. What am I going to do now? He thinks I'm some glamour girl. He'll probably want a pinup picture of me to hang next to Rita Hayworth on his locker."

Paula paid no attention to me. She kept rereading the letter. "This is great," she said. "I'll bet Susanne won't get a letter as good as this. Are you going to show it to her?"

I'd been thinking about the same thing. I was dying to show the letter to Susanne, but something told me I'd better not. "No," I said. "I'm not going to show it to her yet. She'd tell everyone, including my mother."

"If it were my letter, I'd want everyone to know," Paula said.

"Well, I don't. Anyway, not yet. Maybe after I get things straightened out. But how do I do that?"

"Maybe you should send him a picture."

"Paula."

"How about just coming right out and telling him you're a little kid?"

"What would that do to his morale?" I asked angrily. "Didn't you read what he wrote about morale? There's a war on, you know."

"Okay, simmer down," Paula said. "Let me think for a minute." We were both quiet for a little while.

"How about this?" Paula said. "You do it a little at a time, like the clues in a mystery. You start to tell him some things about school or yourself that will give him the idea you're not in high school, without coming right out and telling him. Little by little, he can put it together and figure it out for himself."

"That's it, Paula," I said. "Perfect. I knew I could count on you." I felt relaxed for the first time since the letter had come. I sat back and tried to think about what I would say in my next letter, how I would drop a few little hints, but I couldn't think of one thing. I finally gave up trying. "Like what?" I asked Paula.

"Like the newspaper drive, like the spelling bee. I'm sure they don't have spelling bees in high school. And if you mention that you go to P.S. 132, he's not going to think you're in high school."

"Okay," I said. "I'll do it."

"Can I read it again?" Paula asked.

"Yes," I said. "Out loud."

It was even better to hear it than it had been to read it. I made a face when she came to the part about "small, blonde and cute," but I could almost picture myself as his Kansas cheerleader. It was going to be hard to have to shatter his dream, but Paula was right; I had to do it.

When she finished the letter, I took it back. I put on my coat and walked to the door. As I was leaving, Paula said, "Ask him for a picture."

"I can't," I said. "Then he'd ask me for one."

"Aren't you dying to find out what he looks like?" she asked. "He sounds so cute."

"I'll try to find out," I said, closing the door behind me.

When I got home, I found my mother at the kitchen table trying to teach my brother to knit. I stared at them, not knowing what to think. I'd never seen a boy knitting before. My brother's big, clumsy hands held the knitting needles in an awkward grip, and his face was twisted. My mother stood behind him giving instructions. "Bring the yarn around the needle. Twist it. Now drop the stitch off. No, not that one. You're making a hole."

"What's going on?" I asked, trying not to laugh.

Danny pretended I wasn't there, so my mother answered. "All the eighth-graders, boys and girls, have to knit squares for the War Effort. Your brother is learning to knit."

"I don't see how this is going to help the War Effort," Danny muttered as he dropped another stitch.

"Why do they have to knit squares?" I asked.

"They sew them together to make afghans, to keep the boys warm in cold weather," my mother explained.

Danny looked up, jerked his hand and dropped all the stitches off his needle. "I give up," he shouted, throwing the knitting on the table. "I'll do it later. The guys are waiting for me." And he ran out.

My mother picked up the knitting and got the stitches back on the needle. Her hands flew as she finished the row for Danny. She seemed to be in a good mood, so I decided to take a chance and tell her about the spelling bee and my trip to Mr. Fieldstone's office.

"She sent you to the principal's office?" my mother asked, looking at me with what I felt was new interest.

"Yes."

"And the principal, how did he act?"

"That was the surprise, Momma. He was nice to me."

"He knows she has it in for you because of Danny," she said. "She didn't like it one bit when your father and I went to school about her—and we weren't the only parents. Some people say that had something to do with her leave of absence."

"Mr. Fieldstone told me she has three sons in the service," I said.

"So I've heard," my mother said. "I suppose that would make her nervous."

"So you're not mad at me?"

"Well, that was a very wise-guy thing you said. When I tell you to respect your elders, I don't mean only when they deserve it. You understand?"

I smiled. "I understand."

That night, after dinner, I put a V-mail form in my open notebook so it would look like I was doing my homework. I wrote:

Dear Tim,

Was I excited to get your letter! I never was really sure you'd answer me. The censor took out some parts, but that made it even more exciting in a way because it seemed more real. I go to the movies a lot, and now, when I see war movies, I know I'm going to think of you in some of the parts. I've always been an easy crier, especially at the movies. People near me are always saying "Shh" in the nastiest way. My best friend, Paula, who's in my grade at P.S. 132, says that people change their seats when they see us coming.

The part where you said how the mail from your mother gets you down made me sad. I think that most mothers want to make their children happy, but they don't know how. My mother surprised me today by not yelling when I told her I'd been fresh to my teacher. She was helping this kid who's her pet (my teacher, not my mother) to win a spelling bee and make me lose, and I just lost my temper. So this time my mother was on my side, but most of the time she just doesn't understand. She makes me wear galoshes. Why did I say that? Now you'll picture me wearing galoshes.

Change of subject. Since you told me your favorites, I'll try to see every movie that comes out with Clark Gable or Rita Hayworth in it. I can see why you like her. She's really beautiful and glamorous. But I just can't stand Clark Gable. He looks like he has a snotty attitude. Well, that's just my opinion. I never saw the movie *Angels Over Broadway* because my mother wouldn't let me. Another example of what I mean about mothers.

Every Monday night I listen to "Lux Radio Theater." I don't know if they have it in Kansas, but they get these big movie stars to come on the radio and act out movies they were in. If they can't get the one who played the part in the movie, they get someone else famous. It's great. Sometimes I like things even better on the radio than in the movies, and almost always I like them better than real life. You can imagine people and places more beautiful than they could ever be.

Speaking of imagining, I was wondering, what color are your eyes and hair? And what is it like to live in Dayton, Kansas? I really want to know.

My school is having a newspaper drive for the War Effort.

I have to go now. Tomorrow is a school day, and it's getting late.

Be careful.

Love,
Jeannie

I read it over again to be sure I'd done everything that Paula had suggested. Just to be on the safe side, I added:

P.S. I'm not a cheerleader.

CHAPTER 6

The next morning, I put the letter in my coat pocket so I wouldn't forget to mail it on my way to school. I saw some crumpled newspapers on a chair in the kitchen and picked them up to take in for the paper drive. Just my luck, as I walked out, there was Susanne coming down the stairs. She caught up with me and said hello as if the spelling bee had never happened. I decided I'd act just a little cold, so she'd know I hadn't forgotten.

Paula was waiting for me outside. "I never remember to bring newspapers," she said when she saw us.

"I never forget," Susanne said. It was true. She brought a big stack every morning and every afternoon. Susanne's bar on Mrs. Corey's War Effort contribution graph towered over all the others. No one else's was even close. "When I get the medal, I'm going to wear it around my neck on a velvet ribbon," she said. I rolled my eyes at Paula behind

Susanne's back. We'd heard it a hundred times before.

My books kept falling and losing pages as we walked; Susanne's were held in a perfect rectangle by a leather strap. Her newspapers were neatly piled and tied with a string; mine looked as if I were taking out the garbage.

"Guess what?" Susanne said. "I got a letter from my soldier."

Paula shot me a look. "Can I see it?" she asked.

"I can't get to it now," Susanne said. "It's inside my notebook. I'm taking it in to read to my class."

I knew my letter would never be read to the class, but I had to smile at the thought of it.

"Did you get mail from your pen pals?" Susanne asked us, looking first at me, then at Paula.

Paula said no, and I didn't answer, although I had to bite my tongue to keep quiet. We reached the mailbox, and I quickly dropped my letter in.

"That was a V-mail letter you just mailed," Susanne said. "I saw it. Who are you writing to if your pen pal didn't write to you?"

I smiled but didn't answer.

"You're up to something, Jeannie," she said. "I can tell."

I just kept smiling. I was starting to enjoy it. She'd spend the rest of the day wondering what was going on.

That morning, after the monitors had done their jobs, we went over the homework from the night before.

"Who would like to go up to the blackboard and explain this long-division example to the class?" Mrs. Corey asked.

I raised my hand. She looked right past me. I extended my arm as far as it would go. Vincent DeVito turned around to watch when I started waving my hand around like mad.

"Vincent," Mrs. Corey said, "maybe you would like to answer this question. Or would you like to continue to make eyes at Jean?" As the class made a loud, embarrassing "Ooooohhhh," he walked nonchalantly to the front of the room and copied the example from his homework onto the board. It was right. I figured the reason Mrs. Corey and all the teachers hated Vincent so much was because he was smart enough to find his way out of any mess he got himself into. And he always acted as if he didn't care.

As I watched him return to his seat, Mrs. Corey asked, "And who can give us the definition of *superfluous?*" I slumped in my chair. Her steely eyes fastened on me. "Jean," she said.

"Unnecessary," I answered. *"Too much."* Vincent DeVito turned around in his seat again and smiled at me. If Mrs. Corey had been as smart as she was mean, we'd both have been in worse trouble.

When we finished, Mrs. Corey asked if any of us had received letters from our pen pals. Several hands went up, among them Susanne's and Maxine's. Not mine. I put my hand in my skirt pocket to make sure Tim's letter was still there. I hadn't dared to leave it home where my mother might find it.

"Would you like to share your letters with the class?" Mrs. Corey asked. Hands waved crazily. "We will hear Maxine's letter this morning," she said. "And Susanne, please bring yours back this afternoon. We will try to read one each morning and each afternoon. Come up to the front of the room, Maxine, and please begin."

Maxine unfolded a piece of V-mail stationery and read:

Dear Maxine,

Thank you for writing to me. It is very nice to get mail from the good old U.S.A. I can remember when I was in fifth grade. Do they still teach about South America in geography class? It's very nice that your school is having a newspaper drive. I don't know what they do with all that newspaper, but it's nice that you're helping the War Effort. I'm glad you like your teacher and hope you listen to what she tells you.

Write again soon.

Thank you.

Sincerely,
Jim Foster

I couldn't get over the difference between Maxine's letter and mine. I wondered what Susanne's would be like.

"That was lovely," Mrs. Corey was saying. "What a nice way to start our day. And now I have something I am sure many of you will appreciate." She took some long, narrow sheets of white paper out of her desk drawer, which I recognized immediately as the seed lists.

For country kids, the first sign of spring may be a robin or a crocus, but for us—growing up in Brooklyn apartment houses—it was the seed list we got each March. It listed, I thought, every flower and plant known to man. The prices were low, and the seeds would be delivered to us at school in time for planting in the spring.

As I took the seed lists from Vincent and passed the pile to the kid behind me, I decided this was the year I would get a Victory Garden.

There were a few empty lots in the neighborhood that had been divided into little plots so people could help the War Effort by growing their own vegetables. Last year, my mother had said I was too young to have a Victory Garden, but she couldn't use that excuse this year.

I wanted to plant seeds and watch them grow in neat, even rows. I'd water them all the time and work in my garden with special tools. Then one day, I'd walk into the apartment with my harvest: a bouquet of flowers for my mother, a bowl of strawberries for Dad and maybe a turnip for Danny.

But most of all, I wanted a Victory Garden because it would be a place that was all mine, even if it was just a tiny patch of land.

I spent the rest of the morning working out a plan. I chose a few vegetables and memorized the names of the flowers that sounded best.

I got home for lunch just as the mailman was leaving our building. I knew there wouldn't be any mail for me, but I just couldn't stay away from the mailboxes. Ours was empty. Mrs. Saks was turning the key in hers as I started across the hall to my apartment. I heard a kind of screechy squeal from Mrs. Saks, and I turned and ran back to her. She was clutching a handful of V-mail envelopes and yelping. She grabbed me in a tight hug and shouted, "Mail from Buddy. Five letters." I hugged her back, and we sort of danced around a little. Mrs. Saks was laughing in a way that was the next thing to crying. Susanne came in just then and looked at us as if we'd gone crazy. Then she saw the letters in her mother's hand. She ran over and hugged her mother and me, and we all danced around together.

Other neighbors came to see what all the noise was about, so Mrs. Saks gave Susanne and me each a big kiss and went to tell them.

It was too hard for me to stay mad at Susanne after that. We separated for lunch but promised to walk back to school together.

"Mom," I called, walking into the apartment. "Mrs. Saks got mail from Buddy."

"Thank God," my mother said. Then, "Don't walk in. The floor's wet. I'm putting down newspapers." She'd just finished washing the living room linoleum, blue in the center, with a flowered border, printed to look like an Oriental rug. "Where did I put those newspapers?" she asked herself.

"I took them to school for the paper drive," I told her.

"Then you'll have to wait until it dries," she said. Normally, she'd make a newspaper path for us to walk on. "Tell me about Mrs. Saks while we're waiting," she called from the other side of the living room.

"She got five letters," I shouted back.

"Who got five letters?" Danny asked as he came in from school.

"Mrs. Saks," I said.

"Did they tell where he is?" Danny asked. "Is he seeing any action?"

"I don't know, Danny," I said. "She didn't read them to me."

"You can come in now," my mother said, after a few minutes, "but take off your shoes."

We walked through the living room to the kitchen in our socks and settled ourselves at the table. There was a steamy smell of clothes drying. The indoor rack hung close to the ceiling above the sink and was full of laundry. A few pieces were still soaking in the sink, waiting to be scrubbed on the washboard. Lunch was on the table.

"Did you get your seed list?" Danny asked me, taking his out of his pocket, crumpling it into a ball and tossing it into the garbage. Danny had to keep reminding me that he was a big-shot eighth-grader.

"Yes, I did," I said, placing mine, only slightly wrinkled, on the table. "Momma, please, this year can I buy seeds for a Victory Garden?"

My mother poured milk into our glasses and sat down. "A Victory Garden? Last year, you let the morning glories die."

"That's because I don't like morning glories."

"How do you know?" Danny chimed in. "You never saw one."

"Momma," I said, "make Danny butt out of this. Can't I at least grow something with a pretty name?"

"Such as?"

I was ready. "Such as hyacinths."

"No. That's a bulb. It takes special care."

"Zinnias?"

"You think that's a pretty name?" Danny asked.

"I'll tell you what," my mother said to me, "you're getting older now. You want to grow a Victory Garden? Fine. I could use the vegetables. You show me you can grow morning glories, and I'll buy you the seeds for a Victory Garden."

"It'll be too late," I said.

"If not this year, then next year," my mother said. "It's my best offer. You'd better take it."

"Asters?" I asked.

"Morning glories," my mother said, taking three cents out of her change purse. "It has to be something that can grow in a cheese box on a windowsill. Morning glories."

"You'll see," I said. "I'll grow perfect morning glories."

"That'll be the day," Danny said, but I just ignored him.

After lunch I met Susanne at the door. I told her about the deal I'd made with my mother. "What seeds are you ordering?" I asked her.

"Oh, I'm just too busy with other things," she answered, making me feel about three and a half years old. At least she hadn't sent her seed money to help hungry children in Europe, which is what I was expecting her to say.

That afternoon, after the seed money was collected, Mrs. Corey said, "Boys and girls, I have a very important and exciting announcement." The room became absolutely quiet. "I have just been told that, on June fifteenth, all the fifth- and sixth-graders in our school are going to present a pageant called Friends of All Nations. Each child will dress in the native costume of a child from another land for a program in the auditorium, to which the other grades and your parents will be invited." She paused. "A photographer from the *Brooklyn Eagle* will be there to choose ten children to photograph for the newspaper."

We were so excited that Mrs. Corey never got us calm again for the rest of the afternoon. A pageant! Costumes! Newspaper pictures! What a day!

Nobody was even listening when Susanne read the letter from her pen pal. What I heard was that his name was Nelson, but everyone called him Bubba. He came from New Orleans, and he couldn't wait to get into the real fighting. It was nothing compared to my letter, absolutely nothing. I decided that once I got it all straightened out and could tell my mother about my pen pal, I'd show my letter to Susanne. I knew she'd be green with envy.

I met Paula outside of school. "Did you hear about the pageant?" she asked the second she saw me.

"Isn't it great?"

"And the newspaper picture."

"I know," I said. "We'll be famous."

"What are you going to be?" Paula asked me.

"I don't know," I answered. "All I know for sure is that I want to have a better costume than Susanne."

"Fat chance," Paula said. "Mrs. Saks will sew her a costume that'll make her look like a Rockette."

"At the Radio City Music Hall Christmas show," I agreed. "But still, I want to get into that newspaper picture."

"Any ideas?" she asked.

I shrugged. "How about you?"

"I think I'd like to be French," Paula answered, without even stopping to think.

"What do French kids wear?" I asked.

"I don't know. Berets?"

"That's it?" I asked. "You're going to put on a beret for the pageant?"

"What are you getting so huffy about?" Paula said. "I didn't say that was all I was going to do. I have to think about it."

"I guess I do, too," I said.

Paula and I spent the rest of the afternoon looking through books and magazines for pictures of costumes. Paula cut out a few that she thought might be good, but nothing I saw said to me: Wear this and you, not Susanne Saks, will be photographed for the *Brooklyn Eagle*. I couldn't settle for anything less.

CHAPTER 7

It was while we were looking through magazines that I got the idea for the haircuts. There was an article in *Woman's Day* about beauty make-overs. It showed these Before pictures of plain women with ugly hair and bad skin and how they looked after the experts cut and set their hair and did their makeup. It was amazing.

"I'm definitely a Before," I said to Paula, getting up from her bed and looking in her mirror.

"Me, too," Paula said.

I held my braids up on top of my head, then let them down. I took out the barrettes that held the ends and pulled my fingers through my hair until it hung loose in crimpy waves. "I'm still a Before," I said. "I need a make-over."

"Can kids get make-overs?" Paula asked.

"I don't know," I said. "Probably not. But I know where rich kids go to get great haircuts."

"Where?"

"Best & Company."

"How do you know?"

"Two ways. First of all, the rich kids in school—the ones who live on Ocean Parkway—go there. Second, I was there once."

"You got your hair cut at Best & Company?"

"I just said I was there. I didn't say I got my hair cut."

"So?"

"My Aunt Helen took me to Best & Company to look for a winter coat. While I was waiting for her, I saw the kids' beauty parlor. It's great. It's for kids only. All these rich little girls were getting their hair washed at beautiful white sinks or having it cut by people who talked to them as if they were grown-ups. They had little chairs in the waiting room and kids' magazines on the tables. Every girl who walked out of there looked like a princess."

"I'll bet it's expensive," Paula said.

"I don't know," I said, twisting my hair back into braids. I turned around to face her. "Do you think we could?"

"What?"

"Get our hair cut at Best & Company."

"I doubt it," Paula said.

"It can't hurt to try. And wouldn't it be great if we could? It would be like a make-over for kids."

"I'll ask my mother," Paula said.

"Me, too."

Paula's mother, who had been wanting her to get a haircut for a long time, said yes, so I began nagging and begging my mother. There was one thing working on my side. Her best friend, Shirley, would never allow anyone to cut her little Florence's hair except the beauticians at Best's. I finally wore my mother down. She went to use the telephone in the corner candy store to find out how much a haircut would cost. She was pleasantly surprised by the answer and made an appointment for Paula and me during Easter vacation.

I pictured myself as a totally different person after the haircut, maybe more like a Kansas cheerleader. I thought it would probably even be easier to think of a costume for the pageant after I saw what I looked like with my new hairstyle. I couldn't wait.

To make the time pass faster, I went down to Gruber's and asked for a cheese box. Mrs. Gruber took a few cream-cheese packages out of a wooden box that said BREAKSTONE'S on the side and handed the empty box to me. I went out at four o'clock on a windy April afternoon and filled the cheese box with some of the hard, rocky dirt that surrounded the curb tree in front of our house. And then I started to get impatient. I wanted the morning glory seeds. I wanted a Victory Garden. I wanted to hear from Tim. And I wanted my haircut.

What I got was the flu. On the first day of Easter vacation, I was sick with a runny nose, a sore throat and a cough, which lasted for the whole vacation. I couldn't even have company because I was contagious. I read a lot of books and listened to the soap operas on the radio.

Two days before our appointment date, my mother came back from the grocery store and told me she'd met Mrs. Miller and Mrs. Saks there. "So I told Mrs. Miller that you wouldn't be able to go for a haircut with Paula," she said.

"What did she say?" I asked.

"She said she wanted Paula to have her hair cut anyway."

"Is she going to let her go alone?" I asked.

My mother looked uncomfortable. "Well," she said, "Mrs. Saks heard what we were talking about, and she asked me if Susanne could have your appointment."

"You didn't say yes, did you?"

"I couldn't say no, could I?"

"Yes," I said, tears starting.

"I would have had to spend the money to call to cancel, and then she would have called and gotten the appointment anyway. I just made it a little easier on everyone."

"Not me."

She put her hand over mine. "I really couldn't say no." I knew that if she had, the other mothers would have thought she was a little nutty, but I still felt betrayed.

"I bought you the new Archie comic," she said. Now I knew she felt guilty. She didn't like us to read comics and never bought them. I took it from her and leafed through the pages, but I was so disappointed I couldn't even read it.

When I got back to school, my first day out after the flu, Paula and Susanne had the same haircut—sleek, shiny bangs and a shoulder-length pageboy. They looked adorable. I wanted to die. My long, thick braids seemed even more babyish and out of style than before. I felt I was being left behind. I held the tears back all day at school, but as soon as I got home, I just threw myself on my bed and cried.

My mother came in and sat with her hand on my back. When there was a pause in my sobs, she turned me to look at her. "What?" she asked.

"Susanne got my haircut," I blubbered. "Paula looks beautiful, and I look like a big baby." When I could catch my breath again, I said, "I never know what's going on. One day everyone is wearing bobby socks and saddle shoes, and I'm still wearing brown oxfords and knee socks. And if I got bobby socks and saddle shoes, they'd all change to something else. I know it."

"This is about a haircut and feeling left out?" my mother asked.

I nodded.

"So do you want to get a haircut?" she asked. "I'll take you to Best & Company."

"That's just it," I said, my voice quivering. "It's too late. If I got one now, I'd just be copying them."

"Hmm," my mother said. "Is Bette Davis a copycat because she wears big shoulder pads like Joan Crawford?"

"That's different," I said. "That's just the style."

"So maybe when the third person gets bangs and a pageboy, that will be the style?"

"Not if the third person is me."

My mother left me to finish my cry. When I was done, I took Tim's letter out of its hiding place under my drawer and read it again. There'd been plenty of time for him to receive my letter and write back. Some of the kids at school had received two or even three letters already, although others, like Paula, had never gotten an answer to their first. I wondered if Tim had received my letter, realized I was a kid and didn't want to write to me anymore. But wouldn't he at least write back one last time to explain? Maybe he wasn't writing because he was in the middle of the fighting, and he just didn't have the time. I didn't know which explanation made me worry more. I folded the letter up and put it back.

I walked into the kitchen and found my mother sprinkling clothes for ironing. She'd dip her hand into a bowl of water and kind of wiggle her fingers over the clothes, dripping droplets on them. Then she'd roll them up, and they'd be just the right dampness for ironing. I always liked to watch her do that, although it wasn't as much fun as watching Feldman the tailor, who would take a mouthful of water and spray it between his teeth onto the clothes.

"So," my mother said, "have you been thinking about a costume for the pageant?"

I'd been counting on the haircut to give me an idea. Now I had no haircut and no idea. "I can't think of anything," I said.

"Why don't you wear your mandarin pajamas and go as a Chinese girl? We can braid your hair in one long pigtail and—"

"I'd rather die than walk out in the street in my pajamas," I said.

"So what's your idea?"

"I don't have one yet, but I'm working on it," I said. I was getting nervous, though. Almost all the kids in school knew exactly what they were going to be, and some of them had even started working on their costumes.

The very next day the letter came. My mother didn't see me get it, but Susanne was coming down the stairs just as I put it into my pocket. I couldn't be sure whether she'd seen it or not, but I didn't think she had. It said:

Dear Jeannie,

No time to write now. Will send a long letter as soon as I can. Don't write again until you hear from me. We'll be moving soon. I think of you a lot. Thanks for signing your letter "Love."

Please send a picture. I love your letters.

Love,
Tim

P.S. I noticed your school has a number instead of a name. Is it like a junior high?

It wasn't much, but it was enough to send me into a tizzy. I'd been right to worry. It sounded as if he was either in the fighting or about to be. I knew he'd received my second letter because that was the one I'd signed "Love," but it didn't sound as though he'd caught any of the hints I'd dropped, except the one about my school, and he'd made his own explanation for that. I was pretty much back where I started from, and that was a problem. I knew I'd have to tell him more clearly, but I didn't know how in the world to do it. Now I was even more anxious for his next letter. I wanted to hear that he was all right.

Between the haircuts, my worry about finding the perfect costume and always thinking about Tim, my head was spinning.

That night, I tried to find a new hairstyle. My mother tried to help. But she could make forty suggestions, and I would find a reason to reject each one. She made one last try on Friday morning. I was standing in front of the mirror with my braids undone. My hair hung in crimped zigzags almost to my waist. I grabbed a bunch of my hair and held it over my forehead to look like bangs. "What do you think?" I asked.

It looked hideous, but it didn't change the fact that Susanne Saks was walking around with my haircut.

"Maybe bangs aren't for you. Maybe it's not such a bad thing that you couldn't get your haircut."

She was probably right, but that didn't make anything any better. I went to school the same old two-braided Jeannie Newman as always.

But that day, the seeds came. I opened the little white envelope, looked at the tiny brown specks inside and started to feel a little better. I ran home from school, strained the dirt in my cheese box, smoothed it, watered it, poked holes in it with a pencil and neatly placed a seed or two in each hole. I covered them, patted them down, inhaled the mushroomy smell of the soil, placed the cheese box on my bedroom windowsill and smiled. It felt like the beginning of something.

CHAPTER 8

One morning in May I looked at the dirt in my cheese box and saw a little green something popping through. A few days later, there were six; the next week, twenty. I'd watered them every single day and sat there staring at the soil, encouraging them to come out, and here they were—my tiny tickets to a Victory Garden. I put the box on the outside windowsill of the sunniest window in our apartment. The plants grew slowly but steadily, with pale green heart-shaped leaves.

In the meantime, I was feeling more nervous every day because I knew that everyone else was getting ready for the pageant, and I still didn't have the beginning of an idea. I could hear Mrs. Saks's sewing machine running upstairs, and I figured she was spending hours on Susanne's costume. Susanne made a big thing about not telling anyone what she was going to be.

Paula found a picture in *The Book of Knowledge*

to copy for her French girl's costume. She put on her white party dress, and Mrs. Miller tied a wide pink sash around Paula's hips. She gave Paula her white stockings and bought a big pink ribbon for her hair. When she was dressed, Paula looked exactly like the picture in *The Book of Knowledge*, but why that was French neither of us could figure out.

"Nobody will know I'm supposed to be French," Paula complained, admiring herself in the mirror.

"So tell them," Mrs. Miller said.

"It's supposed to be a pageant," Paula said. "I can't go around saying, 'Hello, I'm French' all day."

"A beret?" Mrs. Miller suggested.

"Not with an outfit like this," Paula said.

We were all quiet for a minute, thinking. "I've got it," I said.

"What?"

"If she carried a French flag, everyone would know for sure." That seemed to satisfy both of them. Mrs. Miller said she could make the flag—a broad stripe each of red, white and blue—out of material she had in the house. That was that.

"So," Mrs. Miller said, "now that we've solved that problem, what are you going to be for the pageant, Jeannie?"

"I don't know yet," I answered. "I can't decide."

"But the pageant is only a few weeks away," she reminded me. "You have to give your mother some time to get things ready."

I knew she was right, and the last thing I wanted was something thrown together at the last minute, but I still couldn't think of anything great, and I wouldn't settle for less. It was driving me crazy.

"Maybe Russian?" Mrs. Miller suggested. "You could wear galoshes and a peasant skirt and blouse, and that would be it. Easy."

"Not Russian," I said. Galoshes? Not a chance.

"How about Hawaiian?" Paula asked teasingly. "You'd just need a little grass skirt and a little halter top and—"

"Not Hawaiian," I said.

"Maybe you want to be French, like Paula?" Mrs. Miller suggested. Paula gave her mother a dirty look, but I quickly answered no.

"You could be Canadian," Paula said.

"Canadian?"

"You could just wear your regular clothes and wave a Canadian flag." I groaned, but Paula thought the idea was hilarious.

When I left Paula's that day, I took out all my magazines and went through them again. There had to be something, and I had to find it soon. But I was disappointed again.

I went to take another look at my morning glories. It seemed to me that the tallest one was starting to lean over a little, so I asked Mrs. Saks for permission to run strings from our windowsill up to her fire escape, so the seedlings would have support as they grew. Mrs. Saks said yes, and Susanne helped me tie the strings.

A few days later, I was spending a rainy afternoon rummaging in my mother's top dresser drawer. It was a hodgepodge of gloves, scarves and souvenirs that I loved to play around in. By offering to straighten it, I got the chance. There was a delicate ivory fan, some sable tails that had once been part of a coat collar, the china bride and groom from my parents' wedding cake and dozens of handkerchiefs scented with sachet. It was a treasure trove. That day, I found a tortoise-shell comb with three long teeth and an open carved design on its high back. It had been tucked all the way in the back of the drawer and wrapped in tissue. In the same tissue, there was a black lace fan with silver sequins sewn on it. I carried them both into the kitchen.

"Momma, what's this?"

"Look what you found," my mother said, taking them from me and holding them to her chest. "I forgot I even had these," she said. "Maybe you solved your own problem. How would you like to be a Spanish girl for the pageant?"

"What?"

"The fan and the comb are from Spain. Grandpa went there when he was a young man, and he brought them back for Grandma. She gave them to me." She tucked the comb into my hair. I felt it standing up about six inches above my head. She went into the living room and pulled one of the long lace doilies off the table, draped it over the comb and pushed me in front of a mirror. The doily fell in graceful lines around my face, like a mantilla.

I looked Spanish. I looked pretty. She put the fan in my hand and showed me how to hold it. I grinned back at my reflection.

"Stay," she said and walked out again. She came back with the shawl that covered the worn spot on the couch and placed that over my shoulders. It was magic. I couldn't believe it.

"What dress?" I asked.

My mother was almost as excited as I was. "I'll sew a red crepe-paper ruffle around my old black crepe dress," she said. "It will come down to your ankles. Perfect." She tried the dress on me and pinned it to fit. I stood on a chair so I could see the full effect in the mirror. I fanned myself. I turned this way and that. I couldn't stop smiling.

My mother left me alone to carry on my romance with the mirror. I posed and preened and tried a few steps of a heel-stamping Spanish dance. Susanne Saks, watch out. Only after I sat down on my bed and jumped up with a yelp because I'd sat on a pin did I finally take the dress off.

A few calm days passed, and then I got my next letter from Tim. It said:

Dear Jeannie,

I don't know if there's been any more mail from you because we've been moving around so much that the mail is all messed up. The war has been happening very fast here. You probably read about it in the newspapers XXXXXXXXXXXXXXXXXXXX

CENSORED

XXXXXXXXXXXXXXXXXXXXXXXXXXXXXXXX

CENSORED

XXXXXXXXXXXXXXXXXXXXXXXXXXXXXXXX

I've had a lot of time to think, and I spend a lot of it thinking about you. I love that you're an easy crier and you cry in movies. I never cry, but sometimes when I think about you, I choke up a little. You seem like such a nice, soft-hearted girl. The truth is, Jeannie, I think about you a lot. I like to picture you going to the movies, going to school, listening to the radio. It helps me to remember that there's another world than the one I'm in here, a world I can come back to. And when I come back, I want to find you. I know that might sound foolish, but it's like what you said about listening to the radio, how your dreams are always better than the real thing. Maybe you're not so pretty, and I know you're not a cheerleader, but none of that matters. I'm no Tyrone Power myself. The important thing is that you're thinking of me.

It's real late at night, and I'm more tired than I've ever been before. Maybe I've said some things I shouldn't have, but I'm going to take a chance and mail this anyway, because I really am starting to care about you, Jeannie, and I hope you'll tell me you feel the same.

Love,
Tim

I shoved the letter in my pocket and ran out of the house. Thoughts were chasing each other around in my head so fast I couldn't grab hold of one. I started to walk and just kept going. I sat down on a curb and read the letter again, feeling myself blush.

Now I knew for sure that he'd received my second letter and ignored all my careful hints. Why hadn't I just come out and told him the truth? What if he really came to find me? I closed my eyes and pictured this handsome soldier knocking on my door. What next? Would he just pass out cold when he found out I was a chubby eleven-year-old, or would he sweep me into his arms and say, "It doesn't matter, darling. I'll wait for you. The seven years' difference in our age is nothing."

I opened my eyes. It was getting too scary for me. I knew I had to tell him who I was, straight out, no more hints. It would be hard, but I promised myself to write the next day. Once the decision was made, I calmed down a little and started walking again, more slowly.

I thought about the part of his letter that said the war was happening fast and about the part that had been censored. Every day the newspapers had stories about jungle warfare on Pacific islands with strange names. It sounded awful, and I was really worried about him.

I found myself in Prospect Park, feeling worn out. The sudden coolness of the air told me it was getting late. I'd have to start back soon. Couples were walking with their arms around each other. A sailor was rowing a boat with his girl on the lake.

I read the letter again. It was clear he was starting to care for someone, and if that someone wasn't me, who was it? I felt myself flush with pleasure as I realized that I was looking at my first love letter.

I got up, folded the letter into a tiny square and started back, still holding it in my hand. I felt miserable and embarrassed at the thought of the letter I'd have to write, but there was something else, too, something secret and delightful. When I reached my block, I could see Susanne going into the house. I slowed down so I wouldn't have to talk to her, but I couldn't help thinking she'd just die of jealousy if she read this letter.

CHAPTER 9

The next morning, when I got to my line in the schoolyard, Susanne was waving a V-mail letter and saying, "Mail from Bubba. He sent me a picture."

"Ooh," her toady, Maxine, said. "Let me see." When Maxine had finished oohing and aahing, Susanne asked me if I wanted to see the picture.

"Sure," I said, and looked at a photograph of a big, beefy, smiling soldier. "Very nice," I said, handing it back to her.

"She's just jealous because her pen pal never wrote back," Maxine said.

"Oh, I don't know," Susanne said, in a teasing voice. "I think she knows more than she tells."

"If she had a letter, she'd be broadcasting it on the radio," Maxine said.

Susanne ignored her. "Do you want to read my letter?" she asked me.

"Sure."

She handed me a worn V-mail envelope. The letter said:

Dear Susanne,

Your letter was real nice. I will try to answer the questions you asked. I did not finish high school. I quit when I was sixteen. I like to mess with cars. In fact, I have one up on blocks in front of my house. My folks are keeping it there for me until I come back. Sometimes I read *Popular Mechanics*. I don't have any hobby that I know of, unless you count the cars. I'm sending you a picture that my buddy took in basic training. I hope you will send me one of you back. Well, that's all for now.

Your pal,
Bubba

When I looked up, Maxine was talking to someone else, and I was alone with Susanne. "He sounds nice," I said when I handed the letter back. But I was thinking about the difference between Susanne's letter and mine.

Her next words broke into my thoughts as if she'd been reading my mind. "You *have* been getting mail from your pen pal, haven't you?" she asked. "I see the way you watch the mailboxes, and I saw you mail a V-mail letter. There's something going on, isn't there?"

I didn't answer.

"You can trust me, Jeannie," she went on. "Why are you trying to keep it a secret? Is it because your mother doesn't know?" When I still didn't answer, she said, "I'd never tell your mother."

"It's not just that," I said.

She squeezed my arm. "I just knew it," she said. "I knew you had a secret pen pal. What do you mean, 'It's not just that'?"

"It's kind of complicated," I said.

"How?" she asked. "Would you let me read your letter? I let you read mine. I swear I wouldn't show it to anyone or tell anyone."

"It's kind of personal," I said, but that only made her more excited.

"I swear on my brother Buddy's life that I won't tell anyone or show it to anyone," she said.

I knew that, no matter what, Susanne wouldn't go back on swearing on her brother's life. And—I have to admit it—I was dying to show her my letter. I took it out of my pocket and handed it to her.

Just then, the second bell rang. "Don't worry. I'll guard it with my life," Susanne said as the line started to move.

"Wait," I said as she moved away, but she didn't hear me. I'd meant for her to read it then and there, not to take it with her. It drove me crazy to have it out of my hands. I'd have to get it back as soon as I could.

As soon as we got into the classroom, Mrs. Corey started a geography lesson. She gave us outline maps of South America and told us to fill in every country, body of water and mountain range. Then she went out, leaving Maxine as the monitor in charge. I had written *Brazil* on the largest space and *Amazon River* on the snaky line and was looking around the room hoping for inspiration when Vincent DeVito turned to show me his map. He'd written *Brooklyn, The Bronx* and *Staten Island* on three of the spaces. I laughed and happened to look over toward Susanne. She was reading my letter under her desk. I tried to signal her to put it away, but she never looked in my direction. I concentrated all my attention on her face. I was pretty sure I saw her eyes widen and her mouth drop open as she read. When she finished, she stared at me for a long time.

"Put it away," I whispered, but she didn't seem to hear me. It looked as if she was rereading it. I was just about to walk over and take it from her when I saw Mrs. Corey at the door. I stared hard at Susanne, willing her to look at me, but she never took her eyes off the letter. "Susanne," I whispered.

She didn't hear me, but Mrs. Corey did. She took the scene in with a glance, walked over to Susanne's desk and held out her hand. Susanne looked up at her like someone coming out of a trance. "I will take that," Mrs. Corey said.

Susanne looked at me. "No," I mouthed. She looked again at Mrs. Corey's outstretched hand and, after a second's hesitation, placed my letter in it.

Mrs. Corey looked down at the address, looked at me for what seemed like half an hour and placed the letter on her desk. "I will see you at lunch, Jean," she said.

For the rest of the morning, I felt as if my insides had been replaced with blocks of ice. My skin was wet and cold, and I thought I might throw up.

I heard nothing and saw nothing until the bell rang for lunch. Mrs. Corey pointed a "you-stay" finger at me and dismissed the rest of the class. She returned to her desk, unfolded my letter from Tim and started to read it.

"Please don't read that," I said. Mrs. Corey glanced up at me, then continued to read. "It's mine, and it's personal," I said. "You have no right to read my mail."

"This is a school project," she said. "That gives me the right."

"It doesn't," I shouted. I couldn't believe I was saying these words to any grown-up, much less Mrs. Corey. I thought of trying to grab the letter away from her, but she was twice my size. I knew I wouldn't be able to do it. Besides, she was finished. She stared at me as she folded the letter.

"What did you tell this poor boy?" she asked.

"Nothing. I just told him about things at home."

"You must have said something to make him think you are someone you are not."

"No," I said. "I tried to explain. I was going to write today to make sure he understood."

"I am sure you were," she said. She removed from her drawer the notebook page she'd taken from me on the first day of school. She slowly unfolded it and smoothed it out, placing it so I could see the words at the top of the page: *How To Be Popular*. "It will not be necessary for you to write," she continued. "I shall write to him and explain everything. You may go."

"Please don't do that, Mrs. Corey," I said. "I'll do it myself. I promise."

"Apparently, you have not been successful so far. I shall do it. Please go."

I knew it was useless to argue. "Can I have my letter?" I asked.

"'*May* I have my letter?' No, you may not."

It was very spooky walking through the empty hallways, past the deserted classrooms, something like the way I felt inside. I was scared. What if Mrs. Corey told my parents? And I couldn't bear to think of how Tim would feel when he got the letter from Mrs. Corey. There was hardly anyone left on the street, but Susanne was waiting for me. "Jeannie," she called. I pretended not to see her and just kept walking.

"I'm very, very sorry," she said.

I still didn't say anything.

"I couldn't help it," she said. "It wasn't my fault."

I couldn't keep quiet any longer. "It wasn't your fault?" I shouted. "Whose fault was it? Mine, for being dumb enough to trust you?" It just figured that the one time Mrs. Corey caught Susanne doing something wrong, I would get in trouble.

We walked along without talking for a while. Then she asked, "What is Mrs. Corey going to do?" I told her.

"She said she was going to write to him—to set things straight," I said in a dull voice.

"Ouch," she said. After another long quiet time, when we were almost home, Susanne said, "That was some letter."

I didn't say anything.

"It was practically a love letter," she said. "It sounds like that boy is crazy about you. My letters from Bubba are nothing by comparison." There it was, everything I'd wanted to hear, but I just felt kind of hollow inside.

"What are you going to do now?" she asked.

"Nothing," I said, fighting back the tears. "Mrs. Corey will write to him, and that will be the end of that." I felt myself flushing at the shame of it.

"Aren't *you* going to write to him?"

"I don't know. It's too humiliating. After he gets Mrs. Corey's letter, he won't want to hear from me."

Neither of us said anything else until we got to our house. When we were walking into the building, Susanne said, "I'm going to tell you something I haven't told anyone else. I'm going to be a Dutch girl for the pageant. I have real wooden shoes and a lace cap."

"Is that all you can think of, Susanne—your costume? I'm in the worst mess of my life, and you got me there. Think about that."

"Well," she said. "I didn't do it on purpose. It wasn't my fault."

"Stop saying that," I shouted. "It *was* your fault. And I hope you trip on your wooden shoes and break your leg."

CHAPTER 10

That night, I did try to write to Tim, but everything I could think of to say sounded stupid. I couldn't sit still. I went to the kitchen. I watered my morning glories. I sat on the bed. I walked into the kitchen again and sat down with a loud sigh. My mother didn't seem to notice, maybe because my father was acting odd, too. He turned the radio dial from one news broadcast to the next. He kept going to the windows and adjusting our blackout shades.

At nine o'clock, I understood why. The sirens sounded for an air-raid drill. My father was an air-raid warden, captain of the wardens on our block. He put on his armband and helmet and got his flashlight. After making sure there wasn't a sliver of light showing from our house, he went out. He looked very important. He had to patrol the street, to tell people to turn off their lights or adjust their shades.

Danny and I looked at each other. We had been

through many air-raid drills before, at school and at home, but there was always a sort of fear.

"Is it only a drill?" I asked my mother, as I did every time.

"Sure," she said. "Couldn't you see Daddy was expecting it?"

"Yes," I said, "but how does he know? Even wardens aren't supposed to be told."

"He has an instinct for it," my mother said, "a feeling. Some people can tell when it's going to rain. Your father can tell when there's going to be an air-raid drill. Now get ready for bed."

I went to my room and fell asleep without writing to Tim.

But as the preparations for the pageant got more hectic and the term was winding down, there were a lot of things I would have liked to tell him. Every time I tried to write, though, it came out sounding babyish and wrong.

The days before the pageant were like the last couple of days before a school vacation. All the kids were twitching in their seats. Even in the morning, nobody could sit still.

Every day before lunch, our class rehearsed an Irish jig, which we were going to perform at the pageant. It didn't seem like we'd ever get it right.

Finally, the day arrived. On the morning of the pageant, I woke up early so I wouldn't have to rush. The sun was shining, and the air was clear and dry. I walked to the window with a jar of water and poured it carefully into my cheese box. By now the plants were wrapping themselves neatly around the lower part of the strings and had changed to a strong green color.

My mother came to stand behind me. "It looks like this time you're going to do it. This year morning glories, next year a Victory Garden."

"Next year?" I said. "The war may be over by next year."

"It's probably too late for this year," she said, "but I'll ask around, see what's what. Now come and get dressed. You don't want to be late for the pageant."

She slipped the black dress with the big red crepe-paper ruffle over my head. "Be careful not to step on the crepe paper," she said as she zipped me into it. It felt scratchy and stiff compared to the cottons I was used to, very grown-up. My mother combed my hair into a smooth, shiny bun on top of my head and pushed the Spanish comb into it. I was glad I hadn't had my hair cut. Then she placed the lace doily over that. Before she handed me the shawl, she said, "I suppose the other girls will be wearing lipstick?"

My heart jumped. I hadn't even thought of lipstick. "I suppose so," I said, trying to sound as if it didn't matter. But I couldn't keep the grin off my face.

"So maybe a little lipstick," she said, handing me hers.

I put it on, concentrating on staying inside the outline of my lips, like a little kid coloring in a coloring book. I couldn't believe the change it made. My cheeks looked rosy; my eyes sparkled. I looked great; that was all there was to it. Even my brother had to admit it.

My mother walked out with me. It was early, and I'd promised to wait for Paula. Jerome from the third floor came out of the building wearing a Mexican outfit with a serape and a big sombrero. Then some kids from up the block started walking past in groups of two or three, in Chinese costumes, Greek, Norwegian, Scottish and others I couldn't figure out. A girl dressed in an Indian sari came out of the building next door, followed by a boy in a Hawaiian shirt with a lei around his neck. It was like being on a Hollywood set.

I heard a sound behind me and turned to see Susanne stepping outside. I had started speaking to her again a few days before—just barely. She walked down the front steps and turned so my mother and I could admire her. I knew she was going to be a Dutch girl and that her costume would be great. But this was just too much. She had long yellow woolen braids on either side of her starched lace cap. Her blouse and skirt were embroidered with flowers in silk thread. Her apron was trimmed with thick lace, and of course there were the wooden shoes, painted with designs to match her skirt. With every step she made that wonderful *clip-clop* sound I had only read about in storybooks. As usual, she was a star.

Susanne waited until Paula joined us, wearing her

pretty dress and carrying the French flag, and the three of us walked to school together. Anyone else would have changed into regular shoes and carried the wooden ones, but Susanne clip-clopped all the way there, slowing us down but attracting loads of attention.

Somehow, attendance was taken, health inspection was done, last-minute instructions and warnings were given, and we were marched downstairs to wait in the main lobby for the pageant to begin. The auditorium was filled with parents and with kids from the other classes, chattering with excitement. Then there was a sudden hush as the color guard marched down the aisle to "Stars and Stripes Forever," played on the piano by Miss Hoffman. I felt proud to see that my brother was the one carrying the flag. The doors were left open so we could join in the pledge to the flag and the singing of "America." Then it was time.

The announcer, Harvey Frankel, in an Uncle Sam suit and absorbent cotton whiskers, made a little speech about Friends of All Nations, and we were on. The parents and kids in the audience applauded wildly as we marched down the aisle and across the stage in our colorful costumes. Each class did a folk dance from a different country. The stage shook with the force of it, and some of the boys tripped over their own feet, but our Irish jig was a big hit. The applause lasted a long time, and someone in the audience kept yelling "Bravo!" but I couldn't see who it was.

All the sixth-graders did a complicated military march; then everyone crowded onto the stage for the grand finale, a medley of patriotic songs, and it was over.

Afterward, the classes were walked to the gym, where we separated to find our parents. It was a while before I saw my mother. Just a second before I spotted her, I noticed the newspaperman choosing kids for the picture that was going to be in the *Brooklyn Eagle*. He had about twenty of them standing in a group near the water fountain. He was trying to narrow it down to ten. Susanne, of course, was one of the twenty; then she was one of twelve. I was standing still, torn between running to my mother and trying to make the photographer notice me, when I felt someone tap me on the shoulder. I spun around to see Mr. Fieldstone standing behind me. Before I had a chance to wonder what I'd done wrong, he asked, "Weren't you selected for the newspaper picture?"

"I guess not," I said, still wondering whether it was too late.

"I'm surprised," he said. "I thought your costume was one of the best."

"Thank you," I said, blushing.

"Do me a favor," he said, "and tell that photographer the principal said he has to be finished in ten minutes because the children have to return to their classes."

I walked over to the photographer as his assistant was placing her hands on Susanne's shoulders. I got the photographer's attention and gave him Mr. Fieldstone's message. He thanked me without looking up. Then he sort of stared at me. When he looked back at Susanne, he said to his assistant, "No. Take her out. Her costume is too professional. I want a homemade look here." He looked at me again. "This one is perfect," he said. "Put her in. Take out Finland and Scotland, and we're all set."

I couldn't believe it was real. It happened so fast. They pulled over a bench. We stood in front of it; the other kids stood on it. Flashbulbs went off. It was history.

What a thrill! No doubt about it. I had wanted to be chosen so badly. I had even wanted Susanne not to be. But I wasn't thrilled with the way it had happened. I felt bad that Susanne had been pushed out so suddenly. I knew how hard it would be for her. She wasn't used to losing.

My mother watched me being photographed, and she beamed at me. I saw Paula smiling and quietly clapping for me, but there was no time for congratulations because the lines were already forming to go back to our classrooms. Maxine joined me as I walked back toward our line. "What did you tell the photographer to make him take Susanne out and put you in?" she asked.

I stopped in my tracks and stared at her. She was wearing what looked like a gypsy costume. "Are you crazy?" I said. "I told him what Mr. Fieldstone told me to tell him—that he had ten minutes to get finished."

"That's not what Susanne and I think," she said.

"What are you talking about?" I asked, but she just walked away. I saw her whispering to Susanne as the line started upstairs.

I wanted to explain to Susanne that I knew how she felt. And I really wanted to make her understand that I had nothing to do with the photographer's decision. I tried to talk to her when we got back to the classroom, but Mrs. Corey yelled at me, and Susanne turned her back.

She spent the rest of the morning with her head down on her desk. After a while, I heard Mrs. Corey ask her if she was feeling sick. Susanne nodded. Then Mrs. Corey asked if she'd like her mother to be called to come and take her home. Susanne said yes and was sent to Mr. Fieldstone's office to wait. Mrs. Corey walked her out with her arm around Susanne. I knew she was faking.

At lunchtime I checked the mailbox. I couldn't seem to break the habit, even though I knew there'd be nothing for me. There wasn't. I went up to Susanne's apartment. I rang the bell for a long time, but there was no answer, so I went down to my apartment.

My mother was all smiles. Even my brother congratulated me, handing me the bouquet of artificial flowers my mother kept on her dresser. I held the bouquet in one hand and made a great sweeping bow with the other. I said, "I want to thank all the little people, my costume designer"—pointing at my mother—"and my errand boy"—pointing at Danny.

Before lunch I went to look at my morning glories again. I knew something was wrong before I got to the window. There was a difference in the way the sunlight came into the room, no shadowy stripes of strings. I ran to the window and saw that my morning glories were gone. The cheese box lay on its side, seeping dirt. I looked down and saw my seedlings on the concrete below, already starting to turn brown. Above, the cut strings were waving from the Saks's fire escape. It took me a minute to understand. It was the meanest, sneakiest thing Susanne could have done. It was like the attack on Pearl Harbor that got the U.S. into World War II. I wanted to cry, tell my mother, tell Susanne's mother and tell Mrs. Corey all at once. I wanted to buy a hundred copies of the *Brooklyn Eagle* and paste my picture all over Susanne Saks's apartment door. I picked up the cheese box, carried it to my room and kicked it under my bed.

When I sat down for lunch, I decided not to tell my mother. For one thing, she was so happy about my success in the pageant. But also, I was scared that if I said anything, the whole story would come pouring out, and I would start blubbering about everything. And I still wasn't ready to tell my mother about Tim.

So I just sat at the table and finally was roused

from my thoughts by my brother saying, "Ma, I think Jeannie's dying."

"What are you talking about?" my mother asked, not turning from the sink.

"Well, she's not eating her lunch. If she's not eating, she must have a fatal disease." He reached across the table to grab my tuna fish sandwich, and I let him. "She *is* dying," he said.

My mother made me eat half the sandwich, and Danny ate the other half in two huge, disgusting mouthfuls, washing the mess down with my glass of milk.

We left for school together. Danny, who was about as sensitive as your average flea, noticed my mood. He asked, "You okay?"

"Yeah."

"Okay. See you later." He ran ahead to catch up with some of his friends, leaving me to walk the rest of the way myself, thankful that I didn't have to talk to anyone.

My mother knew how hard I had worked on the morning glories, so I decided that after school I'd tell her that I took the plants in to class for extra credit. That would satisfy her, and I'd still get a Victory Garden. She would never believe what Susanne had done, anyway.

That was what made me so mad. But I vowed I would get even with Susanne Saks if it was the last thing I did. This was war.

CHAPTER 11

The next morning I knew what my revenge would be, as soon as I saw Susanne on the way to school, sweet as honey, with her neatly strapped books and her pile of newspapers. I was going to take the medal—for collecting the most newspapers—right out of her hands. I knew it would be hard—nearly impossible—with only ten days left. By now Susanne's bar on the newspaper-collection graph had risen off the oaktag and started climbing up the wall above. All the rest of our bars were anywhere from zero to three inches long. But it was the only way I could give Susanne Saks some practice at doing the one thing she didn't do well—losing.

"Hi," Susanne said when she saw me.

"I'm not talking to you, Susanne Saks."

"Why not?"

"You know what you did."

"I don't know what you're talking about," Susanne said. "I didn't do anything to you. You're the one who got me taken out of the picture."

"Liar," I said.

"If you're talking about what happened to your little plants," she said, "I didn't have anything to do with it. I saw an alley cat walking on your windowsill. He probably knocked them down."

"Yeah," I said, "and took a pair of scissors and cut the strings and pulled each plant out by the roots. An alley cat. Just shut up and leave me alone. I have only one thing to say to you, and then I'm really not talking to you. I'm going to get even."

"How?" she asked. "What do you think *you* can do to *me?*"

But I wouldn't answer. She kept asking, and I kept not answering until she finally figured out that I really wasn't going to talk to her and found somebody else to walk with.

I went to Paula's and told her what happened. She couldn't believe it, but of course she believed it. I told her about my plan for revenge. "I know you can beat Susanne," she said.

I started that afternoon. I walked up to the main shopping avenue and went in and out of all the stores there. "Hello. I'm collecting newspapers for the War Effort. Do you have any to spare?" I was surprised at how easy it was. The hard part was getting them home. By the time I'd collected nine or ten, I'd have to make a trip back to drop them off. It was really slowing me down.

On one of the trips, my brother saw me and asked what I was doing. I told him what had happened with the morning glories, making him swear not to tell Momma. He loved my idea for getting even with Susanne. Danny was a Brooklyn Dodgers fan, so he knew what it was like to root for the underdog. "I'll help you," he said.

I couldn't believe it. "You mean you'll actually come and collect newspapers with me?"

"Did I say that?" he asked. "Of course I'm not going to help you collect newspapers. I'm going to ask Momma if she still has my old red wagon in the cellar. If we can find it, that'll make it much easier for you."

He did, and she did, and I set out again, dragging the old wagon. The metal was bent and rusty, but the wheels were in good condition, and it worked. I could load it with maybe twenty-five newspapers before I had to return. At home I stacked the papers in piles against the wall in my room before I started out again.

I was on my third and last trip home with the wagon when I had to wait to let a stickball team in the street finish a play before I could cross. I was so tired I sat down on the curb and watched for a while. When the teams changed places at the end of the inning, one of the outfielders started walking toward me instead of home base. As he got closer, I realized it was Vincent DeVito. He called time and walked right over to me. Everyone was watching.

"What are you doing here?" he asked.

"Collecting newspapers," I said, standing up and pointing to the wagon.

"Who are you, Susanne Saks?"

"No," I said, "and I wouldn't want to be. I'm going to take that medal away from her."

"You are? Why?"

I started to tell him, but his friends were calling him back to the game and saying, "Vinnie, who's your girl friend?" and stuff like that.

"I have to finish the game," he said, "but this is the last inning. Wait for me, and I'll walk you home."

I nodded because a strange feeling in my throat made me think I wouldn't be able to talk normally. I sat down on the curb again and watched Vincent DeVito hit a two-sewer home run and win the game for his team. I saw him glance at me in the split second between the time he hit the ball and the time he started running. I grinned at him and made the thumbs-up sign, and he was smiling as he ran easily around the bases.

When he got back to home plate, all his friends were pounding him on the back and messing his hair and punching him on the arm. I watched as he pulled himself away from them and walked over to sit on the curb beside me. It was, without any doubt, one of the best moments of my life so far.

He stood up and took the handle of the wagon. "So why are you interested in newspapers?" he asked. I stood up, too, and told him while we walked what Susanne had done to my morning glories on the day of the pageant. "I'm not surprised about Susanne," Vincent said. "All that sweetness. You can't trust it."

"No?"

"Nah. You have to ask yourself, am I always sweet and good and nice?" He paused. "Well, are you?" he asked, smiling.

"No."

"That's it," he said, as if that explained everything.

"What's it?"

"She's no different from you and me, only she has to act like she's better. That's the way I figure."

We'd reached my house, and I stood there without talking for a while, thinking it over.

"Are you collecting again tomorrow?" he asked.

"Yeah. I usually go to the movies with Paula Miller on Saturday afternoon, but tomorrow I'm skipping it so I can keep collecting."

"I'll meet you here and help you tomorrow," he said.

I was too dumbfounded to answer.

"Okay?" he asked.

"Okay."

"Ten o'clock?"

"Ten o'clock."

And he was gone.

When I got into the apartment, my mother was waiting with a copy of that day's *Brooklyn Eagle*. There, at the bottom of page twenty, was the picture of the pageant, with me right in the middle. Underneath, it said: *Dressed in costumes representing different countries of the world, these pupils at P.S. 132, Brooklyn, presented a pageant illustrating their conception of the American way.* My mother had sent my brother to the candy store for more copies to mail to relatives.

I studied the picture for a few minutes, but I couldn't wait to be alone so I could think about what had just happened with Vincent. "Wow," I said to myself, "this is terrific," but it didn't seem real.

Did I like Vincent? I didn't know too much about him, really, except that he seemed very different from the boys Danny played stickball with. But he was definitely cute and funny and smart. And he wasn't scared of anything—talking back to teachers, getting marks on his permanent record card, being sent to the principal. In fact, Vincent seemed to live by a totally different set of rules than the ones I followed. Maybe he had more fun.

My mother put her hand on my shoulder. "Are you feeling all right?" she asked.

"Sure," I said, "but I have to bring in the rest of the newspapers." When I'd finished, there were newspapers stacked all around my room, halfway up the walls.

The next morning at ten o'clock, Vincent was waiting on my front stoop when I came out with the wagon. "Hi, Vinnie," I said, blushing. It was the first time I had called him that. He used to be just Vincent DeVito. He didn't seem to notice.

"Let's go," he said, taking the handle of the wagon from me. We collected from stores all morning, talking about movies and radio programs in between. We liked all the same ones. We talked about teachers and the kids in our class. We both liked our old class better than this one. I told him how much I hated Mrs. Corey.

"The trouble is, you're afraid of her," he said.

"Isn't everyone?" I asked.

"I'm not," he said. "I'm not afraid of anyone. I won't let myself be because then I give them power over me."

I was quiet for a moment, trying to understand. I'd never heard anyone in real life, much less someone my own age, talk that way before. Only people on the radio and in the movies did. "Where do you get your ideas?" I asked, wondering how I could get to be more like him.

"I heard that on 'Mystery Theater,' " he said.

When we finished all the stores, we started on the apartment houses. Vinnie waved to a bunch of guys I recognized from the stickball game the day before. "You know, you can go play with your friends if you want," I said, hoping he wouldn't.

"Those guys? Nah," Vinnie said, then stopped. He put the wagon handle down, then picked it up again. "You know, it's funny." He was looking at the ground as he spoke. "The guys from my neighborhood like me plenty, but with you, I feel . . ." He stopped. I could feel the blush rush up to my face. He didn't ever finish that sentence.

I wondered who else he could talk to. I didn't think he had a Paula, and most mothers didn't know too much about the way things were for kids in Brooklyn.

By four o'clock, we were hot, tired and dirty, so we headed home.

When we got to my house, Susanne was sitting outside. As we started to unload the papers, she said, "I know what you're trying to do, Jeannie Newman, but it won't work. I've been bringing in papers since the beginning of the term. You're not going to catch up in a few days."

I didn't answer for two reasons. First, because I wasn't talking to her. And second, because I was afraid she might be right. It would be too humiliating if I didn't win after trying so hard.

Vinnie helped me take the papers into my house and stack them. Piled up, they didn't look like much. "I've got one week," I muttered to myself as I worked. Now I wasn't so sure I could catch up to Susanne. But I was going to try.

The next week was a blur of newspaper collecting. Some days Vinnie came along. After the next Saturday, the stacks of papers were as high as my head, all around the walls of my room and two deep in some places. As I stacked, I wondered if Vinnie would still be my friend when this was over.

When we were finished, we stood back and looked

over my newspaper-lined room. "How are you going to get them to school?" Vinnie asked.

My mouth dropped open. "What?"

"I said, 'How are you going to get them to school?' "

"I never thought of that," I said. The school was closed for the weekend, and Monday was the last day of collection. No matter how early I started on Monday, even if I could borrow more wagons and get friends to help, I could never get all these newspapers in on time. If I didn't think of something fast, Susanne would have the last laugh on me.

CHAPTER 12

My mind kept racing this way and that, trying to figure out how to get those newspapers in to school by Monday.

At dinner I was very quiet. I pushed my food around my plate and pretended to listen to my father and brother talking about baseball. When they'd finished, there was a long silence, broken only by the sounds of eating.

My mother looked at me. "You have nothing to say tonight?"

My brother answered. "She can't talk because she's in love with Vincent DeVito, the worst boy in the fifth grade."

I jumped up to punch him, but before I could get to the other side of the table, my father gently reached for my hand and held me still by putting his arm around my waist. "Sit," he said to me. "Don't pay any attention to him. He thinks it's his job to tease you. So who is this Vincent DeVito?"

I told him about Vincent and about the newspapers. Then I said, "Now I'm not going to win the medal because I can't get the newspapers to school."

"That would be a shame," he said. "I suppose you're trying to figure it out?"

"Yes," I said, "but I can't come up with anything. Even if we got another wagon, and Vincent and I spent all day tomorrow taking them to school, it still wouldn't work because the school is locked on Sunday. We couldn't just leave them out on the street. What if it rained?"

"Mr. Kurtz would have a fit if he came in on Monday morning and found stacks of newspapers in front of the school," Danny said.

"Mr. Kurtz?" my father asked.

"The school custodian," I explained.

"If we had a car—" Danny said. He'd been nagging my father to buy a car since he was old enough to talk.

"A car," I said. "Who do we know who has a car?"

"Not a car—" Danny started to say.

"Uncle Benny," I shouted. "The laundry truck."

"Uncle Benny is running a business," my father said. "He can't take time out to carry newspapers to school."

"Would it hurt to ask?" I said.

"You could ask," my father said, "but if he says no, that's it. No nagging."

"No nagging," I agreed.

"What are you going to do?" Danny asked, teasing me. "Take the subway to Bensonhurst to ask him?"

I was stumped for a minute. "Uncle Benny has a telephone in his house," I said. "Could I call him on the telephone?"

My mother looked at my father. He nodded. "Yes," she said, "you can call him, but not now. He'll get nervous if the phone rings in the evening. Tomorrow you can call him."

I couldn't collect newspapers on Sunday because it rained all day. My mother made me wear galoshes and carry an umbrella to go to the candy store to use the telephone. "First put in the nickel and then wait for a buzzing sound before you dial," she said, handing me a piece of paper with Uncle Benny's phone number written on it.

"Okay," I said, walking out into the hallway.

My mother followed me into the hall to remind me. "Make sure you ask about Aunt Fanny and the boys first."

"Okay, Ma."

As I reached the outside door, I heard her shout, "Make sure to check if your nickel is returned after you hang up."

I didn't open the umbrella when I got outside because the rain felt soft and cool on my face. I walked down to the corner and across the street into Max's candy store. It was dark and quiet inside. There was nobody sitting on the revolving stools along the green marble counter of the soda fountain. Later in the day, Max would be yelling at the teenagers to leave so he could serve sundaes and frappes and ice cream sodas to the paying customers. Now the store was empty except for two little girls trying to decide between coloring books and cutout books and little Diana Corato, with a Dixie cup in her hand, looking into the penny-candy case while her father was using the telephone.

I watched Diana lift the cardboard top off her ice cream cup and lick it clean, first the vanilla side, then the chocolate, until she could see the picture of the movie star on the inside of the lid. "Who's that?" she asked me, showing me a picture of a man in a cowboy suit.

"Gary Cooper," I said.

"Do you want it?" she asked.

"No, thanks, Diana. I have two Gary Coopers. If you ever get a Bette Davis, I could use that."

"Oh, no," she said. "I keep all the ladies. I hate when I get men." She started to eat her Dixie cup slowly and carefully with the flat wooden spoon.

I saw Mr. Corato start to push the folding doors open, and I walked back to wait near the phone booth. Max came over to me. "You're making a phone call?" he asked.

"Yes."

"Is everything all right at home?" Max was a terrible busybody.

"Yes."

"So why—"

"The phone's free now," I said. And I rushed into the booth.

Max pressed his face against the window of the booth. "You know how to use the phone?" he shouted. "You want me to help you?"

I shook my head no, deposited the nickel, waited for the dial tone and started dialing. Max left. I hoped I wouldn't have to ask him for help. The truth was, I hadn't used a telephone before. I'd spoken on one when my parents made the call, but I'd never made my own call.

As I dialed, I started to worry. What if Uncle Benny said no? He couldn't; he was crazy about me. I was his only niece, and he didn't have any daughters. Instead, he had four big, clumsy Saint Bernard–puppy-type boys who never let me play with them because they were afraid I'd get hurt. The few times they were forced to let me play, I got hurt.

My cousin Milton answered the phone. He was surprised to hear my voice and asked if everything was all right. Then he called his father.

"Hello," Uncle Benny said.

"Hello, Uncle Benny. It's Jeannie."

"Jeannie? What's the matter?"

"Nothing, Uncle Benny. Everything is fine. I'm calling to ask you a question."

"So ask."

I remembered what my mother had said. "How is Aunt Fanny?" I asked.

"She's fine. That's what you called on the telephone to ask?"

"No," I said. I drew a deep breath. "Uncle Benny, there's a newspaper-collection drive at my school. I might be able to win the prize, a medal, if I can get all the newspapers I've collected to school on Monday. But there's too much to carry. I was wondering if you could come with the laundry truck and help me."

There was a long silence. I was afraid I'd made a terrible mistake to ask such a big favor of my uncle. When he finally spoke, he said, "This is something you're doing for the War Effort?"

"Yes."

"Of course I'll do it for the War Effort," he said. "What kind of American do you think I am? What time should I be there?"

"Seven o'clock in the morning?"

"Swell. I'll see you then. Tell your mother and father they should be proud to have a kid like you."

I said good-bye, feeling a little ashamed. I knew I was doing it more for revenge than for the War Effort. But I was happy that I would be able to get my newspapers to school. I ran home to tell my family the news.

Later, when the rain had let up a little, I went to try and find Vinnie. When I got to his block, I asked a woman who was looking out her window where the DeVitos lived. She pointed to a small green house near the corner. I walked over and saw

a garden with a lot of roses. There was a tree in the
middle of the yard with a bench built around it. It
looked like the country.

I walked up to the front porch and rang the bell.
I was a little nervous. What would I say if this
wasn't Vinnie's house? What would I say if it was?
A big woman came to the door, all dressed in black,
even her stockings; only her apron showed a little
faded color. I asked if Vincent DeVito lived there.
She said something in a language I didn't understand. Then she went back in the house and closed
the door. I didn't know whether she'd told me to
wait or go away. After waiting what seemed like a
very long time, I turned to walk away.

"Hey," a voice behind me said.

I turned and saw Vinnie coming out of the front
door.

"I thought I was at the wrong house," I said.

"My mother told you to wait," he said, "but she
doesn't speak English. So she told you in Italian."
He seemed kind of embarrassed.

"Oh," I said.

"Don't stand there getting wet," Vinnie said.
"Come sit on the porch." I followed him and sat on
a green wicker rocking chair with a faded cushion.
It was cool and quiet there. The rain made a soothing sound on the roof above us.

When I'd finished telling him about Uncle Benny
and the laundry truck, Vinnie said, "That's terrific.
I'll come and help you load the truck."

I thanked him. Then I couldn't think of anything

else to say. He was quiet, too. It was strange because the day before we'd both had so much to say we'd kept interrupting each other. "I'll see you tomorrow," I said, getting up to go.

"Okay. Tomorrow."

The next morning I was up by six, too excited to sleep. Vinnie was there by six-thirty, and Uncle Benny pulled up on the dot of seven in his big green laundry truck. When he opened the back doors, we saw a space the size of my kitchen, with some white laundry bags lined up along the sides. Uncle Benny pinched my cheek, then went to have a cup of coffee with my parents while Vinnie, Danny and I loaded the truck.

By the time we were finished, the first kids were starting for school. Uncle Benny came out and rearranged a few stacks of papers. "Come on," he said to the three of us, giving my cheek a particularly brutal pinch, "hop in the back, and I'll give you a ride to school."

I was hoping Susanne would be there to see us when we jumped out of the truck at school. She wasn't, but Maxine was, and that was almost as good.

I went into the building and talked to Mr. Kurtz. He offered to lend us the hand truck he used for moving garbage pails. It held loads of papers, so the job was done before the first bell rang. Maxine stayed and watched the whole thing. I knew Susanne would get a full report.

Vinnie and I walked back to our line, jabbering

together. The strange shyness of yesterday was gone. When we got there, I saw Susanne and Maxine talking and sneaking looks in our direction. Susanne had a worried expression on her face. I didn't care that they were talking about us. I knew jealousy when I saw it. All I cared about was winning that medal from Susanne. I didn't know what I'd do if I lost. I could hardly stand the thought of waiting all day to find out.

CHAPTER 13

The day was torture. Mr. Kurtz kept sending for more boys to help with the weighing and measuring until all the boys in our class were gone. I was so nervous I couldn't eat lunch.

They were supposed to announce the winner just before three o'clock. At two-thirty, the suspense was killing me. I left the class to go to the girls' room, but my plan was to peek into the gym, where the tallying was going on. I couldn't get near it. All the doors were guarded. Luckily, I met Vinnie on his way back from helping Mr. Kurtz and asked him how it looked.

"It's still too close to call," he said, "and they've got a lot more to do."

"I'll die if I lose," I said.

"You'll live," he said, making me think he knew for sure that I'd lost.

Just before the three o'clock bell rang, Mrs. Corey told us that the counting still hadn't been completed, and the results wouldn't be announced until the next morning. I could hardly stand it.

When I got home, my mother was waiting outside for me. "Quick," she said, "drink your milk and change your clothes. You got a Victory Garden."

I couldn't believe it. All the plots had been taken long ago. "How?" I asked.

"I met Nettie Fisher in the bakery this morning," she said. "Her Jerry started a Victory Garden, then got accepted to Camp Henry for the summer. He hasn't touched the garden since he heard, three weeks ago. She said you can have it."

I gulped my milk, changed into old clothes and ran out to my mother. I was so excited, I couldn't walk fast enough to the empty lot three blocks away. It had been divided up into twenty plots. Each of them was about the size of five bathtubs side by side. In some of them, people were standing or kneeling, watering or working with tools.

I followed my mother along the path all the way to the back. Jerry's garden was in full sunlight on the side near the fence. It was a mess. The plots I'd passed had neat little rows of plants showing against the brown soil. This was just a jungle of different shades of green.

My mother showed me the difference between a radish leaf, a tomato leaf and a string bean leaf. I couldn't help wishing I'd had a chance to choose my own plants, but I was happy to have anything. She pressed a tomato leaf in her hand and let me sniff. It smelled tangy and spicy, almost like a tomato.

"And what are all the others?" I asked.

"Weeds," she answered. "They have to come out."

I groaned. She was talking about three-quarters of the garden.

"You'll need some tools," my mother said. I walked home with her and came back alone with a twisted fork, a bent soup spoon, a small shovel, my old beach pail and a watering can. I worked steadily all afternoon under the hot sun, pulling weeds, removing stones and waiting in line time after time to fill my watering can from the hose.

Even while I worked I still worried about the newspaper tally. If only it hadn't rained on Sunday, I'd have been sure to win. Now I'd have to sweat it out. But the rhythm of the work was soothing, and sometimes I got so caught up in it that I could forget about Susanne altogether for a minute or two.

More people came to their gardens as the day got cooler—children, women, old men. They worked quietly on their patches.

I was the last to leave, when the light was starting to fade. I collected my tools and turned to take a final look. I could see a garden beginning to take shape. There were four even rows, two of radishes and two of tomatoes, instead of the tangle of weeds I'd started with. The string beans would have to wait for another day, but I felt satisfied, almost calm. Jerry's garden was becoming mine.

The next morning, on the way to school, rumors were flying.

"Susanne won."

"No. Jeannie won."

"It was a tie."

The calm I'd felt in the garden was gone. I was a wreck.

We'd just about gotten into our seats when the door opened, and Mr. Fieldstone walked in, beaming. "Good morning, Mr. Fieldstone," we chorused.

"Good morning, boys and girls," he boomed. "I have some wonderful news. You can all be very proud. A member of your class has won the newspaper drive and will be awarded a medal in an assembly program tomorrow."

We knew that much. Everyone was looking back and forth between Susanne and me. It was like a ping-pong match. My hands were like ice, and my eyes were so wide open I couldn't blink. Susanne looked perfectly relaxed.

"The winner is," he said, and paused like the announcer on a radio quiz show, "Jean Newman." There was a burst of applause. My back was patted; my hand was shaken; congratulations were shouted. Vinnie gave me a smile, a wink and the thumbs-up sign all at once. I felt pretty proud of myself. I'd done just what I set out to do.

Susanne walked over to me, smiling. "Congratulations," she said.

I figured I could talk to her now. "Thanks, Susanne."

Maxine walked over. "You're too nice, Susanne,"

she said, "congratulating her when she only did it to make you lose."

Susanne stared at her for a moment. "Maxine," she said, "I'm surprised at you. I wasn't doing it to win. I was doing it to help the War Effort. I have a brother overseas, you know. What would I do with a silly medal anyway?"

I'd been all puffed up, and suddenly I felt the air go out of me, like an old balloon the day after the party. But in the very next second, I knew, I just knew, that she was lying. I'd won and she'd lost, and the only thing she could do to make herself feel good was to make me feel bad. Well, I wouldn't let her.

"What are you going to do with the medal?" someone asked.

"I'm going to wear it every day for the rest of my life," I said.

It was awarded to me in a big assembly program, which was great. The medal was beautiful, real gold. It was suspended from a blue and yellow ribbon, and I did wear it every day that summer. I used to think Suzanne grew pale whenever she saw it. There was a cash prize, too—five dollars. I knew I'd have to put most of it in the bank, but I was planning to use some of it to buy seeds for my garden.

The rest of the school term was just collecting books, cleaning out closets and washing desks and inkwells. Mrs. Corey even let us bring in books and games. The weather was hot, and no one could stand being indoors anymore. I worked in my garden every day after school, and it was getting better and better. Now it looked as good as any of the others in the lot. I bought more seeds—string beans and carrots, asters and even some morning glories.

The last day of school was a half day. At twelve o'clock, when I got my report card, I saw that I was going on in the same class. I hoped Vinnie would be with me, too.

As our class was standing in line, waiting for the final bell to ring, Mrs. Corey walked over to me. She handed me a brown envelope and said, "I think you should have this. Please do not open it until you get home." I thought it must be something about the medal, maybe how to take care of it. I put it in my pocket.

The bell rang, and we left the building with a whoop. While I was waiting for Paula, Vinnie came over. "Who are you going to have next year, Vinnie?" I asked.

"They have me down for McCarthy's class," he said, "but I'm not going to be here. We're moving in two weeks." His voice sounded flat.

"Moving?" I asked, shocked. "Where?"

"Someplace out on Long Island. I don't know."

"Well, you could have told me before," I said, angry that he'd kept a secret from me and even more angry at the thought of how much I was going to miss him.

"I didn't know till last night," he said.

Now I felt worse for him than for myself. He'd

have to start all over in a new place, making new friends, making sure everyone knew he was the worst boy in the sixth grade. "Can I write to you?" I asked.

"Sure," he said. "Maybe I'll come see you before I go." He turned to leave.

"Vinnie." He turned back. I squeezed his arm, hard. "I'll miss you a lot," I said.

"I'll miss you, too," he said and walked away very fast.

Paula had been waiting for me. "Are you coming home now?" she asked.

"Later," I said. "I want to stop at my garden for a few minutes."

"Do you want me to come with you?" she asked.

"Nah," I said. "I'll come over later."

I walked to my garden and sat down on a big sunbaked rock. I looked at the neat rows of seedlings and thought about how much I'd miss Vinnie. I'd never before had a friend who was a boy, and I'd been wondering if he'd turn into a boyfriend. Now I'd never know. Then I thought about being finished with Mrs. Corey. Suddenly I knew that she must have realized I was smart, or she wouldn't have placed me with the same class next year. That made me feel a little better.

I got up and pulled out a few weeds that had popped up since yesterday. I had to decide where I was going to plant the seeds I had bought. All I knew was that I wanted morning glories along the fence.

That was when I remembered the envelope Mrs. Corey had given me. I took it out of my pocket and opened it. There was another envelope inside, a red-white-and-blue-striped V-mail envelope. My hands were shaking as I pulled it out, glanced at the return address and saw the name *Timothy Haywood*. I tore it open and read:

Dear Mrs. Corey,

 I got your letter. It took me a long time to take in what you were telling me. I was so wrapped up in my own idea that it was hard for me to understand the simplest fact. I know that you think Jeannie led me on, but I'm writing to tell you that she never did. She wrote me the kind of letter any kid might write, and I took it and made it into what I wanted it to be.

I was lonely and scared. I envied the guys who had girls back home. So I took a little schoolgirl's letter and built a fantasy on it. I can't even say I'm sorry—except for the trouble it caused Jeannie—because it kept me going from one day to the next. I think Jeannie understood that, and that was why she never completely straightened me out. But, Mrs. Corey, she never lied either. She just wrote to me about home. I've read her letters again and again, and that's all it was. I guess she even tried to tell me who she was, but I wasn't ready to see.

I think Jeannie Newman is a great girl. She's funny, smart and kind. Please tell her I said so.

Please tell her I said thank you.

Sincerely yours,
Timothy Haywood

Tears spotted the paper as I read it again. The words *great, funny, smart* and *kind* kept repeating themselves in my mind. I thought I liked them even more than *pretty* and *popular*. Yes. Much more.

I ran home and into my room. I pulled out one of the V-mail forms I'd abandoned so many weeks ago. *Dear Tim,* I wrote. *Boy, do I have a lot to tell you—*